Dear Reader,

I've always loved old movies like *Bringing Up Baby,* and *The Lady Eve,* in which the serious hero wants absolutely nothing to do with the persistent heroine. And yet...deep down, he does. Boy, does he.

With that in mind, I thought how fun to reverse that dynamic back into the couple's grade school past, with my heroine as a serious girl wanting nothing to do with my cocky boy-hero, who'd do anything to get her attention. Needless to say, after he grows up and enlists in the air force, he catches her attention without even trying.

Kendra and Jameson work out their conflicts on the beautiful Southern California coast, which I fell in love with after discovering my new husband's hometown of Palos Verdes Estates, on a hill just south of the city. It was second nature to set a romance there.

Hope you enjoy the story. Visit me at www.isabelsharpe.com!

Cheers,

Isabel Sharpe

Back in Service

—

Isabel Sharpe

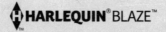

Recycling programs
for this product may
not exist in your area.

ISBN-13: 978-0-373-79775-2

BACK IN SERVICE

Copyright © 2013 by Muna Shehadi Sill

This edition published by arrangement with Harlequin Books S.A.

For questions and comments about the quality of this book, please contact us at CustomerService@Harlequin.com.

® and TM are trademarks of Harlequin Enterprises Limited or its corporate affiliates. Trademarks indicated with ® are registered in the United States Patent and Trademark Office, the Canadian Trade Marks Office and in other countries.

Printed in U.S.A.

ABOUT THE AUTHOR

Isabel Sharpe was not born pen in hand like so many of her fellow writers. After she quit work to stay home with her firstborn son and nearly went out of her mind, she started writing. After more than thirty novels for Harlequin, a second son and eventually a new, improved husband, Isabel is more than happy with her choices these days. She loves hearing from readers. Write to her at www.isabelsharpe.com.

Books by Isabel Sharpe

HARLEQUIN BLAZE
376—MY WILDEST RIDE
393—INDULGE ME
444—NO HOLDING BACK
553—WHILE SHE WAS SLEEPING...
539—SURPRISE ME...
595—TURN UP THE HEAT
606—LONG SLOW BURN
619—HOT TO THE TOUCH
678—JUST ONE KISS
704—LIGHT ME UP
714—FEELS SO RIGHT
761—HALF-HITCHED

To get the inside scoop on Harlequin Blaze and its talented writers, be sure to check out blazeauthors.com.

Other titles by this author available in ebook format.
Don't miss any of our special offers. Write to us at the following address for information on our newest releases.

Harlequin Reader Service
U.S.: 3010 Walden Ave., P.O. Box 1325, Buffalo, NY 14269
Canadian: P.O. Box 609, Fort Erie, Ont. L2A 5X3

To my dear friend and fellow author
Delores Fossen, who patiently introduced me to the
fascinating world of the Air Force.
I am very grateful.

1

"I HAD A great time today, thanks, Crystal." Kendra Lonergan smiled at the attractive middle-aged widow and got a wide smile back. A first! This was good progress. They'd spent the past hour down on Rat Beach tossing balls into the Pacific waves for Byron, the golden retriever Kendra regularly borrowed from a friend for appointments with her dog-loving clients.

"I had fun, too." Crystal bent and stroked Byron's reddish fur. "It felt good to be on the beach again. Thanks, Kendra."

"You are welcome. See you next week!" Kendra tugged Byron's leash and gave Crystal a quick wave before leading the dog back down the block to the Lexus minivan that had belonged to her parents. For a while now she'd been intending to sell the car and buy something smaller, but she didn't ever seem to have time, and wasn't sure what she'd replace it with. In the meantime, it was a nice—if a bit tough—reminder of the family she'd lost. "Up you get, Byron. I'll take you home now."

She unhooked his leash; Byron bounded into the car and settled on the towel Kendra kept on the backseat. What an amazing animal—she never had any trouble with him. His owner, Lena, Kendra's friend since kindergarten, worked typical lawyer hours and was delighted to have Byron out getting exercise whenever Kendra needed him. Kendra had thought about getting a dog herself, but…she hadn't done that yet either.

The Lexus swung smoothly out of its parking place on Pullman Lane in Redondo Beach; she turned it south onto Blossom Lane, heading toward the Pacific Coast Highway and her hometown of Palos Verdes Estates, a hilltop oasis overlooking the vast urban sprawl of L.A. She was back living in the house she'd grown up in, a temporary situation that had stretched on as the weeks and months passed. The house was much too big for one person, but it was stuffed with memories Kendra wasn't yet ready to leave behind.

Climbing the steeply curving roads of Palos Verdes Estates, windows rolled down to enjoy the cool November breeze, she turned up the volume on a Mumford and Sons song she loved, "Little Lion Man," peeking occasionally at the view of Santa Monica Bay, which became more and more spectacular as she ascended.

She left the view behind and turned onto Via Cataluna, then into the driveway of the house where Lena lived with her husband, Paul. Her cell rang, a private caller.

"This is Kendra." She switched off the engine.

"Kendra Lonergan? It's Matty Cartwright."

Kendra blinked, taking a moment to place the name. Matty Cartwright? From Palos Verdes High School? Whom Kendra had last seen years ago? How typical of a Cartwright to think she'd need no further introduction than her name. "Hi, Matty."

"I'm calling to— Oh, uh, how are you? It's been a long time."

Kendra pushed out of the car, rolling her eyes, not in the mood for friendly small talk. She hadn't seen Matty since her sophomore year, when Matty was a senior, and didn't think she'd ever spoken to her. "I'm fine. What a surprise to hear from you."

"I'm calling about Jameson."

Jameson. Kendra grimaced, opening the car's rear door. Matty's younger brother had been in Kendra's grade from Montemalaga Elementary School through Palos Verdes High School. Not her favorite classmate.

She followed Byron to Lena's front entrance, where she fumbled for the borrowed keys in the pocket of her sweatshirt, not really anxious to be having this conversation. "What about Jameson?"

"I wondered if you could work with him."

Kendra froze. *Work* with Jameson Cartwright? As in *help* him? After the way he'd treated her? Byron whimpered impatiently. She unlocked her friend's door; the dog raced toward the kitchen. "Whoa, back up a second, Matty. Where is he, what happened to him and how did you hear about me and what I do?"

A sigh of exasperation came over the line. Kendra gritted her teeth, tempted to tell Matty where to stick her Cartwright attitude.

"I'm sorry, Kendra." Matty gave a short, embarrassed laugh. "I'm not making any sense. I'm just so upset."

Kendra hung Byron's leash in the foyer closet, feeling an unwelcome twinge of sympathy. "It's okay. Just start at the beginning."

The slobbery sound of Byron lapping water came from the kitchen. Kendra wandered into Lena's airy living room, able to picture Jameson Cartwright as if she'd just seen him the day before. Nordic like his whole family—blond hair, blue eyes, high forehead, strong jaw. Yet she couldn't describe him as severely handsome, like the rest of them, because of his one fatal flaw: a wide, sensual mouth more suited to lazy smiles and lingering kisses than sneering and barking orders. Totally wasted on him. He must hate that mouth every time he looked in the mirror.

All through elementary and middle school he'd harassed her pretty steadily, mostly egged on by his odious

older twin brothers. In high school there had been fewer
incidents, since Hayden and Mark had graduated, thank
God. Senior year Jameson had whipped Kendra for class
president, not because he'd run a brilliant campaign, but
because she'd been eccentric, brainy and overweight, and
he was a Cartwright. *Every* Cartwright sibling had been
president of his or her class.

"You know how our family is all in the military." It
wasn't a question.

"Air Force, right?" Pilots going back generations, most
attaining high rank or managing to be heroes of one sort or
another, at least according to the *Palos Verdes Peninsula
News,* which had done a rather gushy piece on the family
some years back that Kendra had skimmed and tossed.

"Jameson did Air Force ROTC at Chicago University.
He graduated last June with the Legion of Valor Bronze
Cross for Achievement."

Kendra interrupted her who-cares eye roll. Wait, this
past June? Kendra had graduated from UCLA and gone
on to complete a two-year master's program in counseling
at California State by then. "He *just* graduated?"

"It's a family tradition to take a year off before college
and travel in Europe. Jameson settled in Spain and...sort
of took two. Anyway, after college, he finished basic officer training at Maxwell Air Force Base, a distinguished
graduate for top marks in test scores and leadership drills."

My, my. How *lucky* Kendra was that she'd never have
to suffer the pain of being so utterly perfect.

She entered Lena's bright yellow kitchen, where Byron
was already lying in his crate, tired out from his frantic
exercise at the beach. Such a good dog. "Then?"

"Then he was injured his first day of specialty training at Keesler Air Force Base, in Mississippi. He tore the
ACL in his right knee and had to have surgery." Matty's
voice thickened. "He's back home in Palos Verdes Estates

on thirty days of personal leave while he continues recovering enough to go back and recover some more."

"Tough break." Why was Matty telling her this? Jameson needed a Scrabble partner? Someone to read him bedtime stories? Kendra closed Byron in his crate and blew him a kiss. "What do you need me for?"

"He, uh…" Matty mumbled something. It was suddenly difficult to hear her, as if she was speaking through cloth. Kendra pressed the phone harder to her ear. "…accident… with a stray…"

Kendra waited impatiently. Stray what? Bullet? Land mine? Grenade? "Sorry, I didn't hear. Accident with a stray what?"

"Cat." She said the word sharply. "Jameson was injured tripping over a cat. On his way to dinner."

Omigod! Kendra clapped a hand over her mouth to keep Matty from hearing her involuntary giggle. Seriously? Not that she'd wish that miserable an injury on anyone—even Jameson Cartwright—but karma must have had a blast arranging that one.

"What a shame," she managed weakly, barely stifling more laughter. *Latest Cartwright's Journey to Hero Status Cut Short in Fierce Battle. Victim's last words: I tawt I taw a puddy tat.*

"You can imagine what this means to a Cartwright." Matty spoke stiffly. "This could end his military career before it even starts."

But how is the cat? Kendra couldn't bring herself to be wiseass enough to ask. Though she couldn't imagine in a million years making a statement like "You can imagine what this means to a Lonergan." Like they were a rare and special breed of humans the rest of the world could barely comprehend. "I'm sure it's been hard."

"It's been awful." Her voice broke, making Kendra feel guilty for being…*catty*—ha-ha. "Jameson is furious and severely depressed. I've called several times. He only picked up once and would barely speak to me. He won't talk to the rest of the family at all. I don't know if he's eating or anything. I've never seen him like this. Can you help him?"

Kendra's laughter died in the face of Matty's anguish. Depression was not a joke, no matter the cause. Kendra had been paralyzed for months after the sudden deaths of her parents mere days after her graduation from college. "How did you hear about me?"

"I was talking to a friend whose friend recommended you. She said you get referrals from doctors and therapists and hospitals, that your work supplements whatever care they're giving people in various stages of grief. That your methods are unusual but effective. Jameson won't accept traditional talk therapy."

"No?" Oh, there was a big surprise. Cartwright men didn't need some sissy talking out of their feelings. Why would they, when it was so easy to punch or ridicule someone and feel tons better about themselves?

"We…weren't exactly raised on sensitivity and openness."

Well. Kendra raised her eyebrows at the unexpected admission, and at the bitterness in Matty's voice. At least she recognized that much. "I'm not sure I'm the right person to—"

"I know what you're thinking."

"You do?" She doubted it.

"That Cartwrights don't have any whining rights. That I'm being arrogant and overprotective looking for professional help for a guy who isn't suffering from anything more than wounded pride. That he should get over himself and deal."

"Uh…" Darn. That was exactly what she'd been thinking. Except the last part. Telling a depressed person to get over it was not generally effective.

"If it was one of my other brothers or my dad, I'd agree with you. There's no way I'd ask you to try to help one of them. But Jameson is different." Her voice softened. "He's always struggled to fit in. I think life would have been easier for both of us if we'd been born into a different family."

Kendra blinked in astonishment. She didn't know Matty at all, but Jameson? Struggling? He'd always seemed to fit the Cartwright mold to perfection—arrogant, entitled, self-centered...should she go on? "Huh."

"I know, you don't believe me. But he's different from the other guys in the family. And that's why this is hitting him so hard. It's worse than just losing out on his planned future. It's like the final proof that he can't cut it. You know? I don't see it that way, and Mom...who knows... but you can bet Dad and my brothers do."

Kendra stood in Lena's living room, phone pressed to her ear, having a very hard time processing this information, given that it contradicted everything she'd ever thought about Jameson.

"I just know that I can't help him right now, and while traditional doctors and therapists might, he won't go, and he really, really needs help."

"What makes you think he'd let *me* help him?"

"He...knows you."

Kendra gave an incredulous laugh. He knew her? He knew how to typecast her, he knew which buttons to push and he knew how to make her feel loathed and worthless. Thank God her parents had been psychologists and had taken time and care helping her through the pitfalls of childhood with her self-esteem intact. "Not very well. In any case, I'm pretty booked..."

"Please, Kendra. I'll beg if you want me to. You're the first ray of hope I've had in weeks." Matty sounded as if she was about to burst into tears. "I haven't slept all night in so long I forget what it's like."

Oh, geez. Kendra closed her eyes, torn between sympathy for Matty and her instinct telling her she wanted less than nothing to do with men like the Cartwrights ever again.

"Just call him, Kendra. Talk to him. If you think I'm overreacting or it doesn't feel right, then fine, you don't have to take him on. We'll go another route. I just don't know what that would be at this point."

Kendra forced herself into motion, letting herself out of Lena's house. Committing to one call was an easy out, not really saying yes or no, which Matty undoubtedly knew and was exploiting. She was a Cartwright, after all.

Maybe Jameson had grown up some. Maybe Kendra had misjudged him all along, typecasting him as he had her. Hard to imagine, but Matty would know her brother better than Kendra did.

"I'll talk to him." She climbed into the Lexus, started back down the hill toward her house.

"Thank you. Thank you so much." Matty's relief was humble and real, no triumph in her tone. "He's housesitting at a friend's condo. I'll give you the address and his cell. Thank you *so* much."

"Sure." Kendra sighed, feeling both noble and trapped. Lena would have a fit when she told her.

"Um. There is just one more thing."

Uh-oh. "What's that?"

"I'd rather you didn't tell Jameson that I'm behind this. Even though he and I are close, he's…a little sensitive when it comes to family right now."

"Meaning he wants all of you out of his face even if you're trying to help."

"That would be it exactly."

Pretty classic depression symptom. Though if Matty's

description of Jameson as the outcast was correct, he could also be protecting himself from the rest of the family's judgment.

Damn. This was almost intriguing. "Okay. I won't mention you. But I'm not sure he'll buy that six years after our graduation I suddenly want to catch up."

"Tell him you're part of a new program the Air Force is trying out for soldiers on medical leave. Or that his commanding officer or surgeon heard of you through some doctor you work with here. Something that leaves him no choice."

Clearly Matty had thought this through. "So I should lie while I try to gain his trust?"

"Oof." Matty whistled silently. "Do you have to put it that way?"

"Can't you get your commander or some general to write a fake letter?"

"Not me." Matty laughed lightly. "I'm not in the Air Force. I'm an actress."

Kendra brought her car to an abrupt halt at an intersection before she realized there was no stop sign; luckily there was no one behind her. "You're an actress."

"Between jobs I sell real estate, but right now I'm in a musical called *Backspace* at the Pasadena Playhouse. I have a small part, but it's a job." The pride in her voice was unmistakable.

"It's an impressive job." Well, how about that. Her parents must have nearly dropped dead. A canker on the Cartwright family tree! And now Jameson injured and out of his training program? A regular crumbling dynasty. "I'll come up with something."

"Thank you, Kendra. Please stay in touch. And send the bill to me. How much do you charge, by the way?"

Kendra told her.

"*What?* You're kidding."

Kendra was used to surprise and had the explanation for her bargain-basement rates ready. "I want my services available to as many people as possible. I'm not in this to get rich. I like working with people, and I don't want to be limited by fees so high that my clients are thinking every second has to count triple for me to be worth their while."

Happily, money was no problem. Great-Grandpa Lonergan had made a fortune in banking in the early twentieth century, and Kendra's ever-cautious parents had had plenty of life insurance on top of that. She would never have to work, though she knew she'd always choose to.

"How about I throw in two tickets to my show?"

"You're on." Kendra pulled into her driveway on Via Rincon and parked outside the garage, gazing affectionately at the white stucco house with the red-tile roof her grandparents had built into the side of the hill.

"You know, what you do is really remarkable."

"Thanks." Kendra shrugged. It didn't feel remarkable. It was her business, and like any business it could be frustrating, boring, annoying, but overall more deeply satisfying than anything she could imagine doing. For many clients who'd experienced loss, grief and loneliness had become so much of who they were, they didn't want to let it go. Proving they still had plenty of life to live and plenty to offer others was about as good as it got.

She took down Jameson's number, punched off the phone and climbed down from the car. Jameson Cartwright, for God's sake. One of the last people she'd ever imagined seeing willingly again, let alone in a situation where he needed her help.

Following the curving brick path from the driveway, she passed her dad's Meyer lemon tree, heavy with still-green fruit, and the jasmine bush bought by her mom, planted clumsily by Kendra and her brother, Duncan. It would burst into fragrant white blossoms in February. She let herself into the house and headed through the small dining room to the spacious kitchen, her mom's pride and joy. Dropping her bag on the hardwood floor, Kendra dialed her best friend's cell. If anyone would enjoy this story, it was Lena.

"Hey, Kendra, what's up, Byron giving you trouble?"

"I don't think he knows how to make trouble." She helped herself to a can of lemon-flavored sparkling water from the stainless-steel refrigerator and pushed through the sliding glass door out onto the deck overlooking their pool, which overlooked their terraced hill lush with her mom's rather overgrown gardens, which overlooked Redondo Beach and beyond that Los Angeles, the Pacific and the Santa Monica Mountains. "It's a different kind of dog giving me trouble. Remember Jameson Cartwright?"

"*Yes.* Ew. Don't tell me he got in touch with you."

"Sister Matty called me. Jameson was injured on his first day of Air Force training last month." She dragged out a chair from the iron table set her parents had bought soon after they were married and turned it toward the view.

"Last month? What's he been doing all this time? I thought everyone in his family ran to the Air Force as soon as they got out of diapers."

"Nope." Kendra sank into the chair and propped her feet up on the railing. "He took two years off to run around Europe. Spain in particular."

"Two years? No kidding. So what did Matty want?"

"She wants me to work with him."

"You're *kidding!* That obnoxious, bullying… How come? What happened?"

Kendra started smiling before she even opened her mouth. "He's depressed because he tore up his knee at Keesler Air Force Base. Tripping over a cat."

Lena gasped, then her shriek of laughter nearly burst

Kendra's eardrum. "Oh, my God! Another Cartwright hero!"

"I know." She was giggling again, guiltily this time.

"Brought down by a pussy!" Lena snorted and chuckled a few more times. "I know, I know, I shouldn't be laughing. I'm sure it's hell for him. No more Mr. Tough Guy, no more hot uniforms and cool planes. Now who is he?"

"Exactly." Kendra tipped her head back to enjoy the eucalyptus-smelling breeze. "Matty said he's seriously depressed."

"Ugh, I bet. So she wants you to fix up his ego and send him back into battle?"

"Yup." Kendra waited a beat. "Maybe with a squirrel next time."

Another shriek.

Kendra laughed with her. Yes, it was horrible to make fun of someone in physical and emotional pain, but Jameson and his twin brothers…it was sort of inevitable. *Reap what you sow, Cartwrights.* "One interesting fact. Matty never went into the military. She's a working actress. I almost got the impression she had some depth."

"No way."

"What's more, she implied Jameson might have some, too."

"You have to admit, he wasn't as bad as Mark and Hayden."

"Not saying much."

"True. I've told you his dad was a piece of work. We'd hear shouting over there all the time. I don't know if he drank or what, but he had a hell of a temper."

"I remember." Not surprising. Most people who grew up bullies had a first-class role model at home. "I said I'd talk to him."

"Of course you did." Lena sighed. "You can't resist trying to fix everyone. I'm not sure this guy deserves you, though."

"I said I'd talk to him. Then I get to decide what to do. I'm curious, to be honest. Don't tell me you're not. You were madly in love with him."

"Only for a few weeks! Besides, everyone was madly in love with Jameson. He was a jerk, but he was a major hottie."

"Not to me." Kendra shuddered. She liked men whose strength lay in kindness and caring, not muscles and manipulation. Lena had married Paul, a slender, dark-haired fellow lawyer—complete opposite of her plump blond energy—who was gentle, brilliant, funny and the nicest man on the planet. Kendra wanted one of those.

"When are you going to talk to him?"

"When I can stomach it. His sister wants me to make it seem like I'm on official business and leave her out of it."

"Smart. If my brother thought I was trying to force him into counseling, he'd refuse on principle."

"Uh-huh. And honestly, I think he's probably mortified. I mean, really, a *cat?*"

"Oof." Lena started giggling again. "I know, I'm terrible. If it was anyone else it wouldn't be so funny. Call me the second you finish talking to him, okay?"

"I promise." She hung up and sat still for a moment, remembering Jameson in grade school, bringing up his wide, smug smile from her memory bank, that weird nervous snickering he did when taunting her, looking back at his hulking older brothers for validation and support.

In elementary school he'd tripped her in the halls, put worms in her lunch, glue in her hair. In middle school he'd spread rumors that she had mysterious rashes, that she was dating a cousin, that she'd had an abortion in eighth grade, that she was being medicated for a mental illness. In their freshman year of high school he'd asked her to the school dance as a joke—pretending he wanted to date the fatty, ha-ha-ha. Then without lifting a finger, he'd denied her the class presidency she'd worked so hard for.

Why was she even considering helping this guy?

Because she, at least, was a grown-up now. Because he was hurting. Because helping people in pain was her job. Because Kendra knew depression, knew how it could sap your ability to get out of bed in the morning, how the idea of having to live the rest of your life seemed an impossibility, how feeling anything but crushing pain seemed a distant dream, sometimes not even worth going after. Didn't matter what caused the pain, the very fact of its existence meant conquering it should be imperative.

After she'd emerged from the worst of her own grief with the support and help of an amazing therapist Lena had dragged her to, Kendra had decided she wanted to help people out of that same darkness.

For her program, she used the techniques that had helped her the most, starting slow and simple—getting out of the house and back in touch with nature, then gradually resuming favorite hobbies and activities and introducing new ones that had no memories attached. And along with that, listening, compassion and a friendly shoulder—repeat as needed.

Could she offer those things to Jameson Cartwright in good faith? She'd need to make sure she didn't just want to prove he hadn't won. To show him how in spite of him and people like him, she'd emerged with self-esteem intact. To parade her slender self, no longer in thick-framed glasses or drab don't-look-at-me clothes. To show him she had the strength to survive worse than anything he'd ever dreamed of dishing out, a tragedy that put his stupid pranks and arrogance into stunning perspective. To be able to confront him in a situation in which, finally, she held all the power.

Kendra would need to check her baggage and her ego at

his door. If she couldn't be genuine in her approach, she'd do neither of them any good.

A red-tailed hawk circled lazily over a fir tree growing partway down the hill, its uppermost needles at eye level where she sat. The bird landed on the treetop, folded its feathers and stood fierce and proud, branch rebounding gently under him.

When Kendra was in elementary school, she'd found a baby hawk on the fire road below their house—how old had she been, seven? Eight? The creature had broken its wing and lay helpless to move, to fly, terrified of the sudden vulnerability.

In spite of his feeble attempts to peck her eyes out, she'd gotten the creature to the house; her mother had helped her transport it to the Humane Society. Kendra had visited often while the hawk healed, naming it Spirit. The staff had invited her to come along when they rereleased Spirit into the wild. She'd watched him soar into the sky and had felt the deep joy that comes from helping a fellow creature heal.

Kendra had thought of that bird often as she'd struggled through the first year after the crash that left her without family except for the much-older brother she'd never had much in common with who lived abroad. And she'd thought about Spirit when she'd decided on her career path, and when she met people made helpless by grief, and when she was first trying to help people who wanted nothing more than to peck her eyes out. Because she knew something they couldn't grasp yet. That there would be a moment when she could rerelease them into the wilds of a renewed life and watch them soar.

She picked up the phone and dialed Jameson.

2

WE LIVE IN fame or go down in flame. The line from the Air Force song played endlessly in Jameson's head. Torture. As if he needed more.

He was stretched out on his buddy Mike's sofa, staring out the window, sick to death of watching TV. Yeah, he'd gone down in flame. Because this sure wasn't fame, and it could only marginally be called living.

At least Mike had his back, letting him stay at his place so Jameson wouldn't have to crawl to Mom and Dad. As if his humiliation wasn't complete enough, moving back home would have about killed him. He'd met Mike at Maxwell during basic officer training, and in one of those stranger-than-fiction coincidences realized he was living in Jameson's hometown with his wife, Pat, who was with her new-mom sister in Reno. Mike had been assigned to train at Keesler in computer communications at the same time as Jameson, and offered his place after Jameson's accident. Couldn't have worked out better.

His cell rang. Again. He didn't look at it. He hadn't looked at it last time or the time before that. It was Dad or Mom or Matty or one of his brothers or a friend. They'd make stilted conversation, Matty and Mom oozing sympathetic cheer, his male relatives masking their contempt with endless advice about how to recover faster than he was, friends who didn't know expressing shock, Air Force friends going on about all the training he was missing.

He laughed bitterly, throat tight, painful weight in his chest, gazing at the sky. Look out there. No clouds. No birds. No planes. A vast nothing, stretching out over the sea. Perfect metaphor for his days since the accident. Over a month of this limbo, first medical leave, now personal. November 4 today, the accident had happened in early September, then surgery, rehabilitation—felt like forever. And it would be if he was one of the unlucky few who didn't recover post-surgery stability in his knee. The Air Force couldn't use a man who couldn't pass their physical test.

He'd done everything right, everything a Cartwright was supposed to do except want to be a flier. He'd majored in computer engineering at Chicago University, a career field in good demand in the Air Force. He'd excelled in his ROTC training, breezed through basic officer training, in both cases earning the friendship and respect of his fellow officers and commanders. His father and brothers were finally looking up to him, in spite of him being the first Cartwright nonpilot. He was on top, poised to continue at Keesler. He'd ace that, too. What could go wrong?

Everything.

He hadn't seen the damn cat, but he'd sure heard it and felt it. He'd gone down, twisting to one side rather than crush the little bastard, and had torn his ACL—his anterior cruciate ligament, to be precise—clean off the bone, and also damaged his cartilage. Badly. One second in time, a moment he'd take back and redo a hundred different ways if only he could. But, as Dad liked to say, life gave you no do-overs. You had to get everything very right the very first time.

The door buzzer rang, making him jump and curse the intrusion and the surprise. He'd been in town a few days and hadn't seen anyone. Only his family knew he was back, and he'd made it clear he wasn't ready for visits from any of them. This must be one of Mike's friends who didn't know Mike was training at Keesler. Where Jameson was supposed to be. Working hard, moving forward.

Two months of stagnation. Many, many more months to come.

He hauled himself off the couch, thinking a shower and shave were a good idea sometime this month—maybe for Thanksgiving—adjusted his knee brace, and limped through the living room and dining area to the front door, where he pressed the intercom.

"Yeah?"

"Lieutenant Cartwright?" A woman's voice.

He stiffened instinctively. Lieutenant? *Oh, man.* He should not be caught by Air Force personnel looking like such a mess. Why hadn't they called first?

He hadn't been answering his phone.

Crap.

But how had she found him? He'd given out his parents' address here in town.

Dad. Doggone it.

"Yes, ma'am."

"This is Kendra Lonergan."

Jameson did a double take. Kendra Lonergan? From high school? She was in the Air Force? He couldn't imagine it. There must be more than one Kendra Lonergan in the world. "How can I help you, ma'am?"

"Just checking in. I've been sent by Major Kornish."

His orthopedist at Keesler had sent someone here?

"Yes, ma'am." He pushed the buzzer so she could enter the building and hobbled into the bathroom, where he splashed water on his face, combed his dirty hair, cringing at the coarse stubble on his face, and reapplied deodorant, ashamed of how he'd let himself go. That done, he hesitated in the doorway, wondering if he could make it into the bedroom for a clean shirt before she got to his door. He was still slow moving, slower than he thought he should be by now, and didn't want to keep her waiting.

Jameson glanced down. Oh, man. Food stains. Clean shirt was a good idea.

In the bedroom, he'd barely gotten his old one off before the knock came, brisk and no-nonsense, four rapid taps.

Hurry. He yanked the new shirt over his head, part of his physical training uniform, and made it back as fast as he could. Bad sign, this continued pain. He tried not to think about it or what it could mean about the success—or not—of the surgery. Not to mention his chances of staying in the Air Force. Maybe he'd just gone overboard on his home exercises that morning.

"Coming." He reached the door and opened it.

Holy moly, Kendra Lonergan.

No, this couldn't be the same woman.

"Hi, Jameson."

He blinked. The voice was the same. It was her. "What happened to 'Lieutenant'?"

"Doesn't suit you." She stared unapologetically with green eyes he didn't remember being so big or so beautiful. She was also taller. Or at least thinner. And without glasses. Instead of the short ginger hair that looked as if her mother had cut it, she'd pulled back a long mass of auburn waves into a casual ponytail. In place of the drab succession of stretch pants and long shirts, she wore a short flowery skirt under layered tops in bright colors.

Kendra Lonergan was a knockout. And definitely not in any branch of the military.

"You look…different." He hid a wince. Could he say anything more inane?

"Huh." She looked him up and down. "So do you."

Yeah, well, tough. It was unfamiliar and extremely unpleasant to be ambushed like this. He'd been raised to be ready for anything at any time. "What are you doing here? How did you know where I was?"

"Dr. Kornish sent me. I told you."

He narrowed his eyes. "What for? What's your connection to him?"

"May I come in?"

"Why?"

"So I can look around. See how you live, how you're doing." With a flourish she produced a clipboard and a pen from an immense purse that seemed to be made of patches of brightly dyed leathers. "So I can report back."

"To my doctor…"

"Kornish, yes," she answered patiently, peering past him. He moved back as she stepped in, to avoid her getting too close. He was not at his best smelling.

"Why doesn't *he* ask me how I'm doing?"

"Because he'd rather hear it from me." She walked through the dining area to the center of the living room, turning in a slow circle, taking in the TV, the rumpled couch and the state of the coffee table, which made it clear he'd been camped out in this room for quite some time. "Nice place. You own it?"

"I'm house-sitting for a friend. Why does he trust you?"

"I'm a professional." She made some notes on her clipboard and moved toward the kitchen.

"Professional what?" He hobbled after her, trying not to stare at the way the flimsy material of her skirt clung to her very fine rear end.

"I help people recover." She peered into the sink at the pile of dirty dishes. Okay, he wasn't at his best. It was none of her business.

"If you're not a doctor…"

Kendra turned back toward him. "I'm not here for your physical recovery."

"No?" He was immediately hit with an image of her

helping him with his sexual recovery, which irritated him even more. "What, then? Spiritual recovery?"

"Something like that." She moved past him, toward his bedroom. He followed, hoping she didn't do more than glance at the bathroom. It was not pretty.

"My spiritual views are private."

"Nothing to do with religion." She stopped at the bedroom door, flicked him a glance and went inside. Jameson hadn't open the blinds yet. Or made his bed. Or picked up his dirty underwear. Well, she'd invited herself in. He owed her nothing. Though he wasn't wild about a description of this mess going into some report.

This was so effed up. "I wasn't expecting you."

"I called. You didn't answer the phone." She left his bedroom to glance into the master bedroom, still gleamingly neat because Jameson hadn't set foot in it.

"I didn't want to talk to anybody." He followed her back into the living room, feeling like a damn puppy now, more and more annoyed.

"Hmm." She planted herself on the black leather chair next to the sofa, looking as if she was going to stay awhile. "That's a problem."

"Why?"

"Because you have to talk to me." She consulted her clipboard. "First tell me how you're feeling."

He folded his arms across his chest. "If this is therapy crap, I'm not interested."

"Just checking in." She smiled too sweetly, green eyes sparkling. It occurred to him he'd never seen her smile at him. Not that this was a real smile. But damn, it lit up the room even so. "Can I have some water, Jameson?"

"Tell me exactly what you are doing here, what you—"

"Oh, sorry, your knee. I forgot. I'll get it."

"Get what?"

"Water."

Right. He stared after her as she disappeared into his kitchen, keeping his eyes resolutely on the back of her head this time. What the hell? Was she deaf? Crazy?

He made a sound of frustration. No, she wasn't crazy. She was Kendra, as she'd always been, totally sure of herself and incredibly determined. She'd driven him nuts all the way from elementary school through their senior year, simply because he'd never been able to rattle her. Apparently nothing had changed.

Moving carefully, he maneuvered himself onto the big chair she'd left—staking his claim, yeah, but it was also easier on his knee to sit there.

"Now." She came back with the water, stopped to peer at a picture of Mike in uniform with his arm around his wife, Pat, then plopped down onto the couch and drank. Jameson found himself staring at her rosy lips on the glass's rim, the glimpse of white teeth, the pale column of her throat working as she swallowed. Kendra Lonergan was in his apartment, looking like temptation itself. Kendra Lonergan. His brain refused to process it.

Finished, she put the glass down between a coffee mug from four days ago and a plastic tray from a fairly disgusting frozen dinner two nights earlier. She lifted the top page of her clipboard and peered at the sheet underneath.

"I would imagine you're feeling pretty horrible about all this. A big change, not part of your plan at all." Her voice was gentle, concerned. "A threat to everything you've worked for your whole life—a career as an officer in the Air Force."

Her compassion pissed him off even more, because it was so tempting to start whining like a baby. "No, no, this is the greatest."

"Uh-huh." Kendra didn't blink. "You're obviously still in pain."

"Nah."

"You sleeping okay?"

"Never better."

"How is your appetite?"

"Outstanding."

"Any weight gain or loss?"

"Neither."

"Energy level?"

"High."

"Sexual function?"

"Hey." He glared at her, wondering what she'd been scribbling on her sheet. "None of your business."

"Okay." She scrawled again.

"Are we done yet?"

Kendra lifted the clipboard to read. "Subject is exhibiting clear signs of depression, including sleeplessness, minimal appetite, weight loss and lethargy."

Right on all counts. How the hell did she know?

"He is also impotent."

Jameson bristled. "I am *not* impotent."

"Don't worry." She turned that sweet grin on him. This time she was really smiling. It made him want to smile back. Or growl at her. Or kiss her. "I won't tell."

"Kendra…"

"Teasing." Her smile grew wider. "I didn't really write that you were."

"You—" She'd gotten him. Fair game. "Is part of your treatment plan to make me want to toss you off my balcony?"

"If necessary." She capped her pen and tucked it back into the top of the clipboard. "How is your family reacting to your disability?"

"Fine."

"How is your dad reacting to your disability?"

He felt a rush of anger, first at his dad, then at her. She

had no right to question him about any of this. "Dad supports me no matter what."

She held his gaze for a moment, then nodded slowly. "That's what I thought."

Jameson swallowed. He felt a loss, almost a betrayal, as if he assumed she'd be able to see through that lie, too, and offer him—

What? A widdle huggy-wuggums?

For God's sake, get a grip, airman.

"How are your brothers coping with your—"

"Disability. They are also very happy for me." His knee was throbbing. He took hold of his thigh with both hands and swung the leg up to rest on the pile of Mike's *GQ* magazines he'd arranged so he could elevate his injury. "I mean they are also supportive. At all times."

"I remember that about your brothers."

Her tone was quiet, but he sensed the steel in it. A pang of guilt lessened his anger. Kendra knew Mark and Hayden. For years he'd been their puppet, admiring their dadlike toughness and what he'd perceived then as leadership. In college ROTC and basic training he'd learned that a true leader inspired and respected his men. That's the kind of leader Jameson wanted to be in the Air Force. A new kind of Cartwright.

But it looked as if he bloody well wouldn't get the chance for nearly another year. Possibly not at all.

He shifted in frustration, causing a landslide in the pile of magazines under his foot. His leg fell, twisting, onto the table with a thud that shot pain from his knee to his hip.

He was dimly aware of Kendra running from the room. She was back beside him so quickly he wondered if he'd blacked out.

"Here you go. This should help." He felt the chill of a cold pack over his knee, then through the lingering haze of pain, the blessed cool of a wet cloth across his forehead and a warm hand on his shoulder. "Should I call someone? Can I get you meds?"

He shook his head, which was clearing rapidly at her touch. He didn't need baby nursing. "I'm fine."

"Oh, yeah, I can tell. You're in perfect shape." Her voice was exasperated. "Here. Let me at least do this."

She sat on the coffee table and gently lifted his leg into her lap, somehow managing not to hurt him or disturb the cold pack.

"What are you *doing?*" He was unnecessarily snappy from the pain and oddly panicky for some other reason he couldn't identify.

"I'm going to aim karate chops at your knee until you tell me the location of the missing computer chip."

What the—

She didn't, of course. He didn't expect her to. But he also didn't expect what she did do. Carefully but firmly, she began to massage his feet through his socks, which, thank God, were clean that morning.

Her touch was magical, finding and tending to places in his toes, the arch of his foot, his heel, places he didn't realize were in such desperate need of attention. Slowly, the tension and pain in his body started to ease, began to be replaced by relaxation and pleasure.

Wait, what the hell was he doing letting Kendra Lonergan touch his feet?

"Uh, yeah, thanks, that's fine. I'm fine."

"Good." She didn't stop, moved upward, tackling the tight muscles of his ankles, his calves, along his shins.

It was helping. Doggone, it was helping. That spot... *there,* oh, yeah.

But it drove him crazy that she still wasn't listening to him, that he felt, once again, out of control around this woman, out of his element. "You can stop now, Kendra."

"I know." She lifted his leg and put it back on the coffee table, leaving his foot and lower leg tingling from the warmth of her touch, aching for more. He didn't like that she'd come into his house and upended everything about his day and body and attitude in less than fifteen minutes.

He wanted her out of here. He wanted to go back to his bad-assed mood, refining his misery to an art. He didn't want to cope with people who irritated him, seeing his current poor showing as a human being reflected so clearly back to himself.

"You can go now. You should go now."

"You think?" She knelt close to him, smelling flower fresh, and put her hands around his thigh, safely above his knee. She started on the tightness his injury caused in his quads and in his hamstrings, loosening the muscles, increasing the blood flow to his leg. Jameson sucked in a breath. Her hands were strong, long fingered, with clear pink polish.

They were very talented hands.

His cock noticed.

He was wearing sweatpants.

Kendra would notice.

Way more humiliation than he should be expected to bear in one day. "Stop, Kendra. Now."

She stopped, looking up at him with a bemused expression. "We're done, huh."

"Done." He dropped his hands into his lap. She glanced at them as she got to her feet. Of course she'd noticed.

"Better though?"

He nodded stiffly. "Thanks."

"Sure." She sat back down, her color high, picked up her clipboard and stared at it for a moment without seeming to register anything. "So."

"So?"

"We were talking about your family."

"No." He shook his head pointedly. "We were finished talking about my family."

"Ah, yes." Her smile was back. "So we were."

"In fact, I think we're finished talking, period."

"No, not yet." She kept the smile on. This woman did not intimidate easily. She did not intimidate at all. He should know that from their past. He'd been prodded into humiliating this girl more than once, though it hadn't ever quite worked out. Deep down he'd resented his brothers' manipulation, of him and of her. A part of him had cheered when she'd refused to play the traditional role of picked-on student. That same damn part was still admiring her now.

"You're on personal leave, waiting to recover, so you can go back to Keesler and be assigned to a desk job until you can pass the physical exam and be cleared again for worldwide duty. Then you'll be able to resume your specialty training."

He clenched his teeth. If she knew it and he knew it, why bring it up? "Yes."

"If your surgery is unsuccessful, you will most likely be honorably discharged. Since you're planning to be a career officer, how would that feel?"

"Super."

"Uh-huh. I thought so." She scrawled something triumphantly. "Okay, moving on."

"How long is this going to take?"

"You have somewhere to go?"

He held her gaze. "This is an intrusion into my day."

"Of…"

"What do you mean?"

"Your day of what? Pain? TV watching? Brooding? Unbearable waiting?"

"Yes." He spoke through clenched teeth. "It's all I have right now."

"Doesn't have to be that way. What are your hobbies?"

"Oh, for—"

"Okay, okay." Her laughter at his exasperation made him want to smile, too. Instead he glared at her, because that was much safer in a way he couldn't quite comprehend and didn't want to. Not while she was in the room smelling like a flower garden and making him hard with a few strokes of her hands, which none of the PTs at Keesler hospital had come close to doing. "One more question."

"Promise this is the last?"

"Cross my heart." She made a graceful gesture that brought his attention to the dark shadow of cleavage at her neckline.

He must be going completely nuts. "Shoot."

She leaned forward, pinning him with her lovely green eyes. He held her gaze, keeping his cold, impersonal, not wanting her to know how she got to him—a weird reversal of their roles in grade school. "What are you most afraid of, Jameson?"

A laugh broke from him. Oh, no. No way. She wasn't getting that stuff out of him. "That's easy."

"Go on." She looked hopeful, but wary. Smart woman.

"I'm afraid..." He leaned forward to match her posture, ignoring the complaint in his hamstring. "That you'll never, ever get the hell out of here."

To his surprise, she burst out laughing, a musical cascade that shone some light into his darkness and made him feel taller, straighter, lighter himself, though he kept from laughing with her, or even smiling.

Kendra stood and laid a friendly hand on his shoulder on her way past him. "I think that was the first straight answer I've gotten all morning. Except about you not being impotent."

"Could be."

"Okay, you win. I'm off. Don't get up."

"Wasn't going to."

She was still smiling, tall and slender and graceful, her legs shapely and strong looking under the short full skirt, sandals with some sparkly metal on them emphasizing the pretty shape of her feet. "Enjoy the rest of your day."

"You bet."

She tipped her head, looking at him mischievously. "It was very interesting seeing you again, Jameson."

"Surreal."

She nodded once, then walked away, the way she'd said his name lingering behind her. The closer she got to the door the darker the space around him felt. In another three seconds she'd be gone and he'd be back with the pain, the brooding, the agony of waiting, his fate in someone else's control.

At the door, she lifted a hand. He clenched his jaw, stifling the absurd desire to stop her.

Then she disappeared through the door and closed it behind her.

Click.

The room went dead, devoid of sound and light and life.

Jameson hauled himself up and limped into the kitchen, his knee still pissed at him for the thumping he'd given it, mood reverting to its earlier foulness, only now it seemed even less bearable. The reason made him angrier and more frustrated and stir-crazy.

He had no idea when or whether Kendra was coming back.

3

MATTY CROSSED THE alley behind the Pasadena Playhouse and stepped through the artists' entrance onto El Molino Avenue. The show had gone well tonight; she was pumped. The usual stage-door crowd had gathered to see the actors emerge, but given that she had such a small part, Matty put on an impersonal smile and didn't even hope to be asked for her autograph. That way she couldn't be disappointed, and the few occasions she had been asked were a real surprise and pleasure.

The night was cool, mid-sixties, she'd guess, a beautiful night to be out. She had a sudden impulse to drive to the ocean, maybe Santa Monica, which wasn't far from where she lived in Culver City. Hang out on the pier and have a drink. Maybe her roommate and longtime friend, Jesse, would want to come with her.

She was digging in her purse for her cell when it rang. Kendra!

"Hey, Kendra, how are you?"

"Fine. Is this a bad time?"

"No, it's perfect. What's going on?" She tried not to sound too anxious, which was hard, considering she was... too anxious.

"Your brother is definitely having a tough time."

Matty grimaced, stomach sinking. "I know."

"But all is not lost. He's in pain, physically, which will

dissipate, and emotionally, which will be harder. But I think—*think*—he'll let me help him."

"And will you?"

Kendra gave a low, dry chuckle that came from somewhere Matty didn't understand. "Yes. I will."

Relief exploded out of her in a long exhale. "*Thank you.*"

"I might live to regret it."

"No, no, you won't. That is…" She laughed breathlessly. "You *will* live, you won't regret it. What will you do for him?"

"First? Clean up the place and cook him some decent meals. Then we'll try getting out to reconnect with some of the world he knows and introduce a bit of a world he doesn't. See what works. It can be a slow process, but he's not past help."

"Oh, my gosh, Kendra." Emotions jammed in Matty's throat. Hearing that Jameson was not in true despair, that he wasn't going to do something crazy like kill himself… ugh, she couldn't even think about it. That wasn't an option. "I have no idea how to thank you."

"Really, don't be too excited. I haven't done anything yet but piss him off."

"Ha!" Matty nodded sympathetically. "That's not hard these days. Even I can do that."

"We'll see if I can get around the mood. I'll give it a try. For old times' sake."

Matty caught the bite of irony. Hmm. There might be something there. "Kendra…did you and Jameson ever date?"

"*Date?* Jameson and me? *God,* no."

"Huh. Okay, sorry." Matty frowned. Pretty violent denial. The main reason Matty had such huge hopes Kendra could help Jameson was because she'd been sure Jameson had had feelings for her back in middle and high school. Maybe she'd been wrong.

"I'll stay in touch and let you know how things are going."

"Thank you. Thank you so much. I—" Matty rolled her eyes. "I can't stop thanking you."

Kendra laughed. "Not a problem. Talk to you soon. Take care."

Matty ended the call and stood, pressing the phone to her cheek, trying to contain her excitement. This could be good. This could be really, really good. She wanted Jameson free of pain, but also free of the family pressure to be something he might not be. She'd done her medical research, she knew ACL repair surgery could be unsuccessful, that there was a small chance Jameson could end up out of a career in the Air Force, the first Cartwright discharged since God knew when.

But maybe for him that wouldn't be the worst thing in the world. Maybe Kendra could help him rediscover living life his own way, as he'd been doing in Spain, working for a U.S. company, taking art and English courses at St. Louis University in Madrid and dating a dancer, before their father had reached his patience limit and dragged him back to the U.S. and the Cartwright Plan for Life.

A hand bumped her arm. She automatically moved away.

After that, Jameson had—

"Mattingly?"

Matty's head jerked up. Only one person outside her family ever called her by her full name.

Her eyes met a pair of deep brown ones under a shock of wheat-colored hair that had gone slightly gray at the temples. Somehow she managed to stifle a gasp.

"Chris." *Calm. Stay very calm.* As if she'd just bumped into him a week ago, not wrenched herself away from him back…how long had it been now? Years. She'd been a senior at Pomona College. He'd been an associate professor. Bad choices had happened. Drama. Pain. Deep love, and the best sex she'd ever had. Not that she was comparing. "What a surprise to see you."

Surprise was putting it mildly. If she didn't make sure to keep breathing, she'd pass out on the sidewalk.

Luckily, being raised by Jeremiah and Katherine Cartwright had taught her how to suppress every vestige of human emotion. Not a good technique on stage, but it could come in damn handy during real life.

"I saw the show." He seemed calm, too. But then, he always did. Except when he was laughing or about to come. "You were great."

Matty accepted his compliment with a polite nod. She had a few solo lines and part of one song—no bragging rights, but she took pride in having been chosen for that much, and in doing her role well. God knew she never took any theater job for granted. "Glad you enjoyed it."

"It was…" He was looking at her too intently, with eyes that were too warm. "It was a shock to see you, Matty, I admit."

"A good one, I hope." She was appalled at the automatic response. *Do not flirt, Matty.*

"Best one I had all week." He smiled down at her and boom, too many memories came rushing back—the nights of passion, the blissful stolen hours together.

What the hell? Had she learned nothing?

"Chri-i-is?" A woman's voice behind them, fake sweet. "*There* you are."

And there she was, slim and elegant in some high-fashion drapey tunic thing she pulled off to perfection. Exactly the type Chris should be with.

"Zoe, this is a former student, Matty Cartwright. Matty, this is Zoe Savannah."

Matty nearly snickered. *Zoe Savannah?* She was perfect. Right down to the leopard-print pants.

Smiling with as much warmth as she could muster, Matty chided herself. Zoe had every right to date Chris. She was closer to his age, for one thing—*meow.* And she was probably a lovely person. Or maybe she wasn't and they deserved each other. Either worked. "Nice to meet you, Zoe."

"Oh, me, too! I *loved* the show." She whacked Chris playfully on the arm with her program and went into gales of laughter for no apparent reason. "And now I see why Chris was staring at you all night. He knows you! I was afraid it was love at first sight."

Actually, it had been.

"No, no, nothing like that." He glanced uncomfortably at Matty, who refused to look uncomfortable.

"You look great, Chris." She wasn't lying, unfortunately. He looked incredible, hair still thick, that new sexy touch of frost at the temple. He'd always reminded her of a cross between Ben Affleck and Russell Crowe: boy-next-door handsome but with powerful masculinity backing it up. "Still teaching at Pomona?"

"They haven't fired me yet."

They should have when she was there.

"Silly." Zoe whacked him again. "You're tenured."

Matty smiled again, for real this time. She was happy for him. He'd wanted that very badly. "Congratulations. A great accomplishment."

"Thank you, Matty." He really needed to stop looking at her like that, half amused, half hungry. It was horrendously unsettling.

"Well!" She glanced pointedly at her watch and lifted a hand in cheery farewell. "I'm due to meet someone for a drink. Great to see you, Chris, and to meet you, Zoe."

Not waiting for answers, she turned and headed for her

red Kia Sportage parked in the lot behind the theater, her cheeks hot, mind whirling. So. Finally, it had happened. She'd seen Chris Hamilton.

For the first couple of years after graduation she'd imagined bumping into him, fantasized about it, actually. How after one glance into her eyes, he'd tell her he'd made a terrible mistake letting her go, that he couldn't live without her, that he loved her desperately and always would and blah blah blah blah.

More years had gone by, six in total by now, and she'd stopped worrying about seeing him. Stopped worrying she'd fall apart, beg him to take her back, stopped worrying about the pain she was sure only he could bring. Because she was over it, thank you very much. There'd been other men since, and no, she was not comparing.

The only really awful part was that after all her efforts, after she'd reached a real understanding of the forces that drove their passion, analyzed that passion to death and accepted not only that it was over, but that its being over was for the best, tonight it turned out Chris Hamilton in the flesh was still dangerously attractive to her. Whatever had pulled them together, in spite of the utter stupidity of professor and student hooking up, that power was still there.

"Matty."

Crap. Matty closed her eyes, considered pretending she hadn't heard him, but he wouldn't buy it. Probably because it was ridiculous.

She whirled to face him. He stopped short, watching her warily. Damn him, why hadn't he put on weight or wrinkled or just turned ugly, for heaven's sake? He looked fabulous. Six feet of good-looking that knew how to do the sheet tango better than anyone she—

No, she was not comparing.

"What do you want, Chris?" Matty bit her lip, shocked

at how bitter and angry she sounded. So much for putting her feelings safely behind her.

"I want to see you. I want— I just want to see you."

"Ha!" The syllable came out without her permission, a mixture of shock, horror and a tiny explosion of pleasure. "How does Zoe feel about that?"

He put his hands on his hips, pushing back his jacket. Stomach still flat. Thighs still long and muscular under casual pants. Darn him.

"Zoe is a colleague."

"Oh, so you're doing those now, too?"

"Low, Matty." The bastard spoke calmly. She could not get to him with insults.

Matty checked herself. She should not *want* to get to him at *all*.

"Sorry. You know me. If it's in my brain, it comes out my mouth." She inhaled slowly to settle herself. "I just don't think getting together is a good idea."

"But…how is that possible?" He looked genuinely confused. "I only have good ideas."

Her laughter was reluctant. Charm as well as sex appeal. Chris had it all, the slime bucket. "No, thank you."

He took a step toward her.

Turn around. Turn around and walk away now.

"You look great, Matty." His gentleness enveloped her. Too much intimacy. "I like your hair long."

"Yeah, thanks." She was not going to tell him how fabulous *he* looked.

"You doing okay?"

"Yes! Fine! Great!" Her voice cracked. He'd notice. He was good at that. And what woman wasn't a sucker for a man who noticed? It's just that *she* hadn't noticed six years ago, that while she had fallen madly in love with him, he was only interested in what lay between her legs. "I'm getting theater work pretty regularly, and I have a side business in real estate that's picking up."

"Good. Good for you." His brows drew down. He pursed his lips, the way he did when he had something uncomfortable to say. "I've thought about you a lot over the years."

Me, too. She stood silent, hands in her jacket pocket clutching her car keys.

"Well." He touched his forehead as if he were tipping his hat and turned away, a gesture at once so familiar and dear to her that tears threatened. *Six years ago, Matty. For God's sake.*

She walked rapidly toward her car, breaking into a run when her steps weren't getting her there fast enough.

Damn it. *Damn it.* What the hell was wrong with her? How could she let him affect her so deeply?

She unlocked the car, wrenched open the door and hurled herself inside, started the engine and peeled out of her parking space.

Santa Monica Pier, here I come. She was going to go there alone and drink herself into a stupor, how pathetic was that?

Very! And it was exactly what she was in the mood for. A long parade of drinks, surrounded by happy partyers and the wild, wavy ocean. She'd sit by herself, looking mysterious and sultry, indulging memories she hadn't allowed herself to call up for years, brooding and wallowing in emotional agony.

Then she'd sleep soundly in the apartment she shared with her best friend and be fine tomorrow. Chris would again be safely part of her past and she could really move on this time, having gotten this first post-relationship encounter over with and ending up unscathed.

An hour later, she was standing at the pier's end, inhaling deeply, pulling her jacket around her for warmth against the stiff, salty wind. Of course she was much too sensible to get drunk. One beer and the crush of bodies around her had gotten annoying, the noise not conducive to proper misery. Her big scene, like most, played better in fantasy than in real life.

But she loved it out here, staring at the black sea, a whole world under there, not one single resident of which had gotten his or her heart crushed by Chris Hamilton.

They'd met in class her senior year. He was teaching a seminar on music and culture in Paris around the turn of the twentieth century. She'd thought he was hot from the first day. In fact, she and her girlfriends—including a new friend named Clarisse—had giggled and oohed and aahed and had a great time dissecting his every word, gesture and look. As crushes went, hers seemed particularly intense, but so what? He was a professor. She was a student. And never the twain shall sleep together.

They'd gotten to know each other through a shared love of all things French, had talked earnestly after class one day, then another, had gone out for croissants and café au lait. Then lunch at a French restaurant he particularly enjoyed…

Later they'd admit that they'd known what was happening, but since they hadn't the slightest intention of doing anything about it, the attraction was harmless. What counted were the ideas they shared, their similar views and tastes and humor.

Ironically, the crossing of the line had happened because of Clarisse's first "suicide attempt," a low-risk grab for attention after a guy dumped her.

Eventually, Matty had realized Clarisse suffered from pretty serious mental issues. Compulsive lying, sociopathic tendencies and a deep need to screw her friends' boyfriends. But at the time, Matty had been terrified and extremely upset. Who wouldn't be? The woman had tried to take her own life!

Matty had called nine-one-one and ridden with Clarisse to the hospital. When she'd heard Clarisse was going to survive—of course she was—Matty had finally broken down, tears that wouldn't stop. Walking home to her dorm, she'd run into Chris, returning from a Pomona orchestra concert. One look at her face and he'd invited her out for coffee. She hadn't wanted to be out in public looking like hell. No problem, he'd drive her to his apartment, where he'd set up the spare bedroom if she wanted to stay over. They'd shared a bottle of wine. Talked until very, very late.

She'd never made it to the spare bedroom.

The next morning they'd agreed it could never happen again. They weren't that kind of people. He was too old for her—more than ten years older. She was his student. An affair was wrong, and he could lose his job. They'd stay away from each other.

They couldn't stay away from each other.

For the next six months they'd tried to break up, gotten back together, then did both again. All those agonies of longing and pain followed by the joys of giving in to temptation, the guilt, the fear—by the time Clarisse caught on and set her sights on Chris, Matty was frankly exhausted. When she'd caught them together, along with the pain there had been relief. Finally it was truly over. No more temptation. Because Matty understood what he was and how foolish she'd been.

Chris had come after her, he'd explained. He'd laid the blame on Clarisse. It wasn't what it looked like, he'd sworn to her...

Please. It was always what it looked like.

Three weeks later, Clarisse took enough sleeping pills to look ill, but not really threaten her life, and Matty had known it was over for them, too. She'd waited, even telling herself she shouldn't, but Chris hadn't come looking for her again.

On the pier now, arms wrapped around herself, squinting into the wind, Matty thought about how she'd come such a long way since then. She'd built a good, rich life for herself. Dated a couple of guys seriously, though none who took her over the way Chris had.

Yes, she was comparing. She'd always been comparing.

But unfairly. Her feelings in college had been intensified by her youth and inexperience, by the lure of the forbidden, by the perfect bubble in which their encounters took place. She hadn't met his friends, he hadn't interacted with hers. They'd had no problems to cope with but the drama of their own taboo passion.

A tear made its way down her cheek. She flung it forward into the sea, sniffed angrily and turned to go home.

Enough. She'd done what she'd come here to do. Brooded. Remembered. Cried one beautiful tear. The actress side of her had been fed.

Now she'd do her father proud, march home, get up at 0700 hours and take on the next day of her life.

4

KENDRA PULLED INTO the parking lot at Villas of the Pacific, CD player blaring Adele's "Don't You Remember." Villas? Really? She could have sworn they were apartment buildings. Nice ones, yes. But a villa needed a sprawling estate. Jameson didn't quite fit that mold, but he'd also looked painfully out of place in his friend's apartment, which was decorated with modern art, odd sculptures and plants. Jameson belonged in a more traditionally masculine interior, all leather and dark wood, books and model fighter jets, one plant, always about to die...

She found a visitor spot and turned off the engine, sat for a moment in the sudden silence, annoyed at herself for being nervous. Hadn't she been through all this after her visit here the day before? Yes, she had. Going forward she'd continue bypassing Jameson's obnoxious behavior, understanding that it came from his pain and anger. She'd focus only on how she could help him. And she'd ignore the...complication.

Finding herself a teeny, tiny bit attracted to Jameson after all these years did not mean the world was about to end. He was an attractive man. So what? He was also an entitled jerk, who happened to be in a terrible situation and needed Kendra's help. Kendra had agreed to help him because...quite honestly, she was curious. Who was this guy now? Who had he always been? Why had he chosen *her* to make miserable for so long?

One thing she had definitely decided—no more massages. Yikes. Not that his erection had been significant. He was a guy, one who probably hadn't had any in a long time. His reaction had undoubtedly surprised him as much as it had her, especially after so many years of rather juvenile enmity between them.

Out of the car, she took a moment to gaze over the red-tiled roofs and palm trees toward the rust-colored cliffs that dropped to the edge of the vast Pacific. Blue sky today, a good breeze—the sight calmed and filled her as it always did. She could bring beauty and positive feelings and hope back into Jameson's life if he would let her. She'd focus on that. The erection, not so much.

Today's goal: clean the apartment, cook him a healthy meal. Push him gently to talk about his situation. Duck when he threw things at her. Maybe throw a few things back.

Kendra turned to unload the groceries and cleaning supplies she'd brought for this visit, one bag of each. Above all, she'd stay cheerful and brisk in spite of his sarcasm and cranky bad-boy mood, intent on what she was there to accomplish. She was not the same cowed high school kid having to fake self-confidence. She had the real thing now.

At the entrance to Jameson's building, she balanced one bag on her hip and the other on a raised knee, trying to free up a hand to push the buzzer. Her finger had almost made it when a guy pushed out the door and let her in with a warm smile. Well. Looked like she'd catch Jameson by surprise again. She'd called that morning and left a message after another client canceled a late-afternoon meeting, letting him know she'd have time for him today. He hadn't called back to say he wouldn't be in or didn't want to see her, so here she was.

On the second floor she turned right and strode down the cream hallway, enlivened by dark green carpeting and prints of landscape paintings on the walls. At his door she balanced the bags again and knocked, four fast raps, *I'm here, ready or not,* then stepped back to wait, bright smile in place.

Nothing.

Was he home? Had he planned to be out just to annoy her?

A noise inside. Her heart gave a little flip and she scoffed at herself. *Still scared of the big bully, Kendra?*

The door opened.

Whoa.

Jameson had cleaned up. Gone was the stubble, ditto the greasy hair and wrinkled clothes. He looked really good.

Really good.

Unwrinkled navy-and-white Air Force T-shirt over neat khaki shorts. Great legs, scarred on one knee. Awesome chest.

Had she referred to him as an attractive man?

She'd lied. He was smoking hot.

And he was standing there, stone-faced, staring at her. Was she gawking? Well, *yeah,* but she didn't think it was that obvious.

"Come in." He stepped back to let her pass.

"Hello, Jameson." She pushed through the door. First thing that hit her was the absence of crap strewn all over the living room. "Wow, you cleaned."

"Mike has a service." He seemed taller today? Maybe he was just standing straighter. In any case, he already looked 100 percent better, and Kendra hadn't even started her program yet. Matty would be happy.

"Looks like you resumed your human form." She smiled at him, cheerful nurse, big sister, teacher, counselor, whatever kind of person would not want to have wild sex with him all over the apartment. "Did you get my message?"

"What's in the bags?" He took one from her, apparently possessing at least some gentlemanly tendencies.

"That's cleaning stuff, obviously not necessary now. This one is groceries."

"I've got food."

"Not this food." She took the bag into the kitchen, aware of him limping after her.

"So, what, you're taking over my life now?"

"Every bit of it, yes." She put the bag on the counter and started unloading. He was still playing cranky, but his tone didn't sound quite as bitter as the day before. More progress. "How's your knee today?"

"Better than ever."

"Still in pain, huh."

"I love pain."

"*That's* lucky." Always the tough guy. Funny how grief affected people so differently. Some closed up, like Jameson. She called those Turtles. Others, like herself, plunged into activity to alleviate in others what they were suffering themselves. She called those Avengers. Then there were Pancakes, utterly flattened by the experience, and Curators, who turned their memories and memorabilia into museums of those they'd lost, and on and on. "Your home exercises going well?"

"Yes, ma'am."

"Good." She didn't really need to ask. His type would want to get better as quickly as he could. Athletes, military, anyone who depended on his or her body would be driven to stay in the best shape possible and didn't mind the work it took to get there.

She'd just try not to think about how his body was already in the best shape possible—broad shoulders, flat stomach, long legs, no doubt impressive muscles all over...

Ahem. Kendra had a job to do, and it didn't entail standing around imagining Jameson Cartwright naked.

"I'll make you a basic spaghetti sauce. You can eat some, freeze the rest when you're sick of it. You like to cook?"

"Haven't done much lately." He seemed huge in the small kitchen. She'd have to get him sitting on the other side of the counter so she didn't bump into him every time she moved.

"It's easy. I'll show you. You can make this. Anyone can make this."

She pointed to the ingredients neatly laid out on the counter. "Ground beef, carrots, onions, tomato puree, beef broth and cream. Want to chop onions?"

"Chopping onions will help me come to terms with losing a year of my life, Kendra?"

She gave him another unreturned smile, not surprised by his sarcasm—she'd heard it all—but shocked by the jolt of sympathy. That was a switch. She'd spent her grade school years, coached by her parents, vainly trying to feel sorry for Jameson Cartwright when she didn't want to, and now she was feeling sorry for him automatically— though she still didn't want to. "I think you'd be surprised what can help."

He shrugged. "You're the expert."

"That is so true." Kendra found a cutting board already out on the counter and selected a knife from the magnetic strip next to the sink. She'd spent last night researching ACL surgery and the recovery process. Long and slow, the worst kind of sentence for a man like Jameson. Nine months, on average, to recover normal use of the knee— though many people were never back to 100 percent—and often pain lingered after that. "You know how to chop onions? If you don't, I'll show you."

"I know how."

"Yeah?" She pointed to the chair by the stretch of counter that doubled as a table. "Have a seat there. I'll pass you stuff to do."

"Yes, ma'am." He sat.

"Did you help your mom in the kitchen?" She passed him the board and knife.

"Sometimes."

"She a good cook?"

"Average."

Kendra turned back to the sauce ingredients. Yes, she was getting one-word answers, but at least he was answering, and no sarcasm this time. One of her clients had been so depressed, Kendra would show up at their early appointments and pretty much talk to herself.

"My mom was an amazing cook." She ripped open the red plastic net holding the onions. "Always experimenting with other cuisines. We had Thai food, Indian, Chinese, you name it."

"*Was* an amazing cook?" For the first time, his voice lifted to a normal conversational tone.

"Yes." Kendra put a large onion down on the cutting board in front of him. The news of her parents' deaths had been pretty big locally. Ken and Sandra Lonergan had been active in the Palos Verdes Estates community and in the schools. She would have expected Jameson to hear somehow, even having been away at college in Chicago. But maybe he didn't have long catch-up chats with his parents the way Kendra had had with hers. Or maybe he'd heard and forgotten, since it wouldn't have meant much to his life. Hard to imagine sometimes, since it had pretty much imploded hers. She understood so well when clients said they'd wake up day after day, surprised the sun was still shining. "My mom passed away a couple of years ago."

"I'm sorry." His words were clearly heartfelt.

"Thank you." She couldn't look at him, still found it

hard to speak when she talked about the accident. "Chop the onion whatever size you want. Doesn't really matter."

"Okay."

She set about peeling carrots, feeling his eyes on her, her throat still tight. Music would help. Kendra generally liked an uplifting soundtrack around clients to mitigate silences when they occurred and lessen the pressure to produce constant conversation. "Does Mike have any CDs?"

"Yeah, I think in the cabinet under the TV." He was already on his feet, hobbling into the living room.

Well. Doing something nice for her. Another hint that he was capable of pleasant behavior. Unless he was terrified Kendra was about to do something girlie and horrible, like cry. "Thanks, Jameson."

"Uh-huh."

She turned back to her carrots. Baby steps…though it bothered her he was still limping two months after surgery. Maybe it was the nasty jolt he'd given his knee the day before when she was here, but by now he should be able to—

A horrific blast of death metal came over the speakers. Kendra yelled and jumped, then flung herself toward the kitchen door to peer into the living room. He could not be serious.

The music went off. Blessed silence.

"Uh." Jameson was grinning, crouching in a rather painful-looking position in front of the CD player. "That was not on purpose."

"I am glad to hear that." She put her hand to her chest, this time smiling genuinely instead of in polite encouragement. He was ten times more handsome when he wasn't scowling, though he managed to turn even the grouchy look into an appealing bad-boy aura.

But this…if Kendra didn't already know her heart was pounding from the scare, she might think he was affecting her. But, um, of course it wasn't that. "I think they play that music in hell."

"Wait." He actually chuckled. "You know this CD?"

"God, no."

"It's called *Satan's Soundtrack.*" He held up three fingers in a Scout's-honor pledge. "Not kidding."

"Nice." She stepped farther out of the kitchen toward him. "What's the band called?"

"Flagrant Death Meat."

Kendra cracked up. "You aren't serious!"

"I am." He held up the CD, chuckling.

"That is just too weird."

Their laughter trailed off. Their gazes held. He stayed crouched. She stayed in the doorway. A dozen yards apart, they might as well have been chest to chest.

Kendra swallowed. Moments of intimacy with her clients could be important. Sometimes they allowed people the safety to talk about something real. All she wanted to do was hurl herself back into the kitchen to escape Jameson and the strong pull he exerted.

He turned abruptly to the TV cabinet. "I'll find something else."

"Great, thanks." Kendra fled to the sink, shaken by her inability to take charge of the moment. She could not back down from a connection that might prove helpful to Jameson. That was the core of her practice—inspiring trust, creating a safe environment into which clients could dump their innermost fears and feelings.

Instead, Kendra had stared at him as if he were a bug pinned to a foam board.

The smooth strains of an entirely different type of music filled the apartment. The Lumineers. Just the right atmosphere.

"Better?" Jameson limped back into the room and took his seat.

"Much, thank you."

Chopping and peeling sounds filled the kitchen. Kendra took a deep breath, determined to get back on track. "Have you been out of the house since I saw you?"

"'Go outside and play. Get some fresh air.'" He did a high-voiced mom impression.

Kendra cracked up. "Your mother?"

"That's her."

She peered at him over her shoulder. She'd always imagined Jameson as an outdoor type, playing ball with his brothers, building forts, killing things... She couldn't remember much about Katherine Cartwright. Just an impression that she was a good deal younger than her husband. "What did you want to be doing indoors instead?"

"I dunno."

"Yes, you do."

He sent her an annoyed glance. He was chopping the onion with such painstaking care that she almost started giggling.

"Need a ruler?"

"You got one?" He *almost* smiled.

"Tell me what you did inside at home when you were a kid."

This time he didn't bother answering, just looked completely disgusted.

Kendra turned back to her chopping. "Did you listen to music? Write stories? Play with action figures? Watch TV?"

"Not TV. Not in our house."

"No? What, then?" Kendra waited, pushing the carrot peelings down the disposal. Jameson would talk or he wouldn't. At least he was thinking about the answer. "How about I ask you again what you're most afraid of? You seemed to love that question last time."

He made a sound of exasperation. "I'm actually most afraid you'll keep asking me that until you like the answer."

"You can count on it." She rinsed her hands in the sink, dried them leisurely on a San Francisco Giants hand towel.

"I liked to draw."

"Yeah?" she answered calmly, cheering inside. Score one for Kendra. She'd schedule that in as one of their activities. Maybe they could combine a beach trip with a sketching session. "Were you any good?"

"Probably not."

She'd bet he was. Guys like Jameson wouldn't bring up something they were bad at.

"I took art classes at St. Louis University when I lived in Madrid."

"You were enrolled there?" She started searching for a grater in Mike's cabinets, keeping her voice casual, as if she were only politely interested, to keep him comfortable and talking.

"No." His response was quick and tinged with bitterness. "I did AFROTC at Chicago University. But all us kids took a year off to travel before college."

"What a great idea." She opened another cabinet.

"I took two."

"Why?"

"Because I'm so special."

"I knew that about you." Kendra pulled a gleaming box grater triumphantly from the back of the next cabinet. The thing had probably never been used. "Why two years?"

"One wasn't enough."

"I can imagine." She spoke offhandedly, picked up the carrots. "Fun times."

"I wasn't ready to start life yet."

"I see." She set up the grater opposite him on the counter, dying to press him further. Not ready to start life or the Air Force? Why the delay? "What was her name?"

"Marta."

"Wait, really?" Kendra sent him a surprised look. "I was actually kidding."

"I'm not." His voice turned a little wistful. Kendra picked up the carrot and started shredding it viciously, appalled to find herself annoyed. What the hell? She liked to think of herself as the soul of emotional generosity. If Jameson had found the love of his life in Madrid, that was wonderful.

"Onion's chopped." He pushed the board toward her. "What's next?"

"You still in touch with her?"

"You think that's your business?"

"Not in the least." She finished the carrot and scooped the shreds onto the cutting board next to his neatly chopped onion, brought them both over to the stove. "I've never been to Spain. Tell me about Madrid."

"Great architecture, art, food, people. I got a part-time job in an English bookstore, took classes and mostly did what I wanted."

"Big change from high school and living at home."

"Yeah. I loved it too much. Dad had to come get me, to remind me I had a future, which I couldn't spend living in the moment."

"Sounds like a parent." She turned to grab the hamburger as an excuse to see his face. "But for the sake of argument, why couldn't you?"

"Because, Kendra." He held her gaze, his smile growing slowly. "That's not what Cartwrights do."

"I got that impression." Kendra nodded calmly, weighing whether it was smarter to keep pushing now or pull back. And whether she should stand there staring into his blue eyes much longer, because she was going to start thinking about him naked again. She turned and pulled out a large saucepan from under the sink.

"I'm not in touch with Marta."

"As you said, none of my business." She felt herself coloring. A tiny tense spot loosened in her chest. *Kendra, you are strictly forbidden from getting crushes on clients.* "Any idea where the olive oil is?"

"Try that cabinet?" He pointed.

She found the oil and added a glug to the pan, waited until it was shimmering to add the onion and carrot.

"What did *you* do after high school?"

Kendra suppressed a snort. *Recovered from you, you expletive.* "I went on to UCLA, majored in psychology."

"Ah." He came to stand next to her, watching her stir the vegetables. She wished he'd sit back down again. His nearness was so…near. "So you followed in the parental footsteps, too."

Funny, she'd never thought about it like that. "I guess I did. The difference being that they didn't expect or demand it."

"Right." His face shut down. She'd pushed too far there. Matty's assessment of her brother's uneasy relationship with the Cartwright legend seemed accurate.

Interesting.

"So now we add the hamburger and stir until it's not pink anymore. You want to do that?"

He took the wooden spoon she offered. Kendra stepped back, grateful to put distance between them, and watched as he broke up the meat and let it brown, music wafting in, harder to hear with the sizzling on the stove, but a nice atmosphere, warm and good smelling. She hoped he was enjoying it.

Beef browned, she added the tomatoes and broth, put the lid ajar and set the sauce to simmer.

"That'll be an hour or so. When was the last time you left this apartment?"

He put his hands on his hips, looking down at her. "You don't want to know."

"I didn't think so." She wanted to take a step back, but there was nowhere to go unless she could dissolve into a cabinet. "You up for a short walk? It's beautiful out today."

He looked skeptically toward the window, where twilight was threatening.

"There's enough light for a stroll around the grounds here, on good level paths. We can go to the beach another time, when your knee is stronger."

"How many times are there going to be? Why wasn't I told about this?"

She tipped her head back to see his face. "Is hanging out with me that awful?"

For another of those electric moments, he looked down at her without speaking. Kendra felt her control of the situation slipping again into a déjà vu sensation that left her mildly disoriented. Honestly. This was not the way her appointments were supposed to go—or had ever gone. Her job depended on her ability to ask this kind of question without caring so much about the answer.

"It's hell, Kendra." He shook his head slowly. "I've never known such agony as having to spend time with you."

She broke into a giggle. "Call me Satan's soundtrack?"

"That's you."

"It's about time I tortured *you* for a change." She thrust a finger toward his chest.

In a case of painfully exquisite timing, the CD ended and the words she'd blurted out hung in pure silence. *Nice one, Kendra.* First rule of her profession: do not make anything personal or take anything personally. She'd done both.

"Hmm." Jameson's eyes narrowed. His hands crept onto his hips. "I guess you do owe me."

"No, no, of course not." She waved his words away, face turning red. "That was just kid stuff."

"Just kid stuff?" His left brow moved up half an inch; his eyes had taken on a particular...warmth that she responded to by heating up herself. "You think?"

"Of course. What...else?" Instinct told her suddenly and firmly that she did not want to follow this line of questioning. Everything she said was turning intimate in a way she didn't understand.

"I wonder sometimes." He was half smiling now, mysterious and I've-got-a-secret. Once again in control while she struggled with bafflement and confusion.

Kendra turned back to the stove, pretending to check on the sauce, adjusting the flame though it didn't really need to be adjusted, thinking that for the first time since she'd started her practice two years earlier, and despite the experience and confidence she'd gained in that time, she might be in over her head.

5

JAMESON TURNED OFF the treadmill in the apartment complex workout room, grabbed the towel from around his neck and mopped his face. Pathetic that a fast walk could make him break a sweat. Granted, it was too warm in the room, and he'd done the full range of exercises his physical therapist had assigned him plus a few more. Don't overdo, yeah, he knew, but he was itching to get back to full mobility. His knee could almost straighten now, and nearly bend to ninety degrees, but it still hurt like a… thing that hurt a lot.

Research on the internet was not encouraging: pain lasting a year, continued swelling and stiffness, some lack of mobility. Worst case the knee would remain unstable or he'd injure his ACL or meniscus again. Second surgeries were deemed "not as successful," which was doctorspeak for "you're screwed, buddy." He was still having pain from overextending his knee when it fell on the coffee table, in spite of the icing and the rest.

Yeah, okay, maybe not enough rest.

Still, today he felt a little better. A little lighter, a little less as if the weight of the world was trying to crush his chest. Looked like Kendra's "treatments" might be working, though not the way she intended.

He couldn't stop thinking about her. She'd certainly knocked him for a loop when she'd walked into his borrowed apartment two days ago, so cheerful and sweet smelling when he was neither. But last night he'd found himself tempted to back off that anger, to really talk to her, open up, lean a little, confide in her.

Because during the evening as they'd cooked together, he'd found a new piece of the puzzle that was Kendra Lonergan, one he'd tried to figure out all through grade school, when she'd first started fascinating him.

She could be vulnerable.

Her less-than-ideal embodiment of femininity and who-cares attitude had made her an immediate target for him in elementary school, egged on in middle school by his somewhat apish brothers, who'd caught on to his interest, which they'd interpreted as disdain and cheered him for wholeheartedly. But Kendra had confused them, too. She hadn't played the geek role, hadn't been submissive to them or to their arsenal of standard bully weapons against her—chief among them being Jameson.

At that age, like every other boy on the planet, he'd looked up to his brothers and father as male role models. He'd been cruel to Kendra as a matter of course, because they dared him to, because he wanted their approval, because he was insensitive and stupid and bristling with hormones.

But she had never reacted the way he or his brothers had expected, with pain or humiliation, tears or pleas to leave her alone. Neither had she pretended the Cartwright brothers didn't exist. Instead, she'd looked at them with what seemed like genuine pity. In those moments Jameson had been the one embarrassed, ashamed of what he'd tried to do. Instead of stopping, giving up, admitting he couldn't get to her, he'd just tried harder, turned his own suffering into bigger and meaner anger.

Kind of like he was doing now.

Through elementary school, middle school and just over the border into high school, their ongoing battle of wills had become one of the strangest relationships he'd ever had. Sometimes he'd wondered, if she'd once, just once, given any sign acknowledging that he existed as other than a pathetic pain in her ass, he might have stopped, might have approached her differently, as something besides a Cartwright menace.

But she never had given in. By high school, he'd been at least slightly more mature, and getting sick of the game. His brothers, trying one more time, had had him ask her to the freshman spring dance as a joke. He'd agreed, feeling sick inside, and at the moment of asking, promised himself that if she said yes, he'd atone for his cruelty by going through with the date, no matter what it cost him.

She hadn't. She'd laughed in his face. Why would she want to go anywhere with *him?* Then she'd walked off, still laughing, calling to her friend to come listen to the latest.

That had been it. He was done. Mortified and relieved. When Mark and Hayden had called on him to plot their next move, he'd said no and hadn't budged, enduring taunting and a few punches for his insolence. That had been the first time he'd stood up to his brothers, the beginning of his emergence from boyhood.

Unfortunately, he'd been destined—or doomed, was more like it—to get to Kendra once more. Senior year, he'd beaten her for class president. She'd clearly run the better campaign on issues of assigning homework based on GPA—the higher your grades, the less homework you'd have to complete—and other substantive ideas. Jameson had swept to victory on a promise of new vending machines, later curfews for dances and the Cartwright name.

A hollow victory. He'd served that whole year with the

sickening certainty that he hadn't earned and didn't deserve the votes or the presidency.

After all that—Kendra still wanted to help him. She was still a fascinating woman. One he was increasingly attracted to.

Back upstairs, he showered and settled onto the couch with ice on his knee. His workouts took an hour or so out of his day. Meals took another two. The rest—boredom and inactivity, doubly intolerable after the busy, active days of basic officer training.

Maybe he should rent a car. He hadn't bothered because of the pain and the expense, but he might go out of his mind if he stayed between these walls for too many more days.

His cell rang. He peered at the display. Matty. He should answer her call. His dad and brothers were easier to avoid, though he'd mistakenly picked up earlier and spoken to Hayden in Germany, so he'd had to hear about all the friends Hayden knew with ACL injuries who'd been back to 100 percent in about thirty seconds and what was wrong with Jameson's wimp ass?

Thanks, Hayden.

"Hey, Matty."

"Jameson! You've been avoiding me, you pig."

"Sorry."

"I know, you're having a tough time." Her tone reminded him exactly of his mom's when one of her boys got sick. She probably had that same pout-frown on, too.

Drove him nuts.

"I'm *fine*."

"Right! Right, of course. You're fine."

Jameson grinned at her loud raspberry. It was about as easy to B.S. Matty as it was Kendra. Namely, not at all. "So what's going on?"

"Nothing. Getting close to selling a house. Still doing

the show. What's going on with you? Are you feeling better? Any improvement?"

He wanted to tell her about Kendra. She probably didn't even remember Kendra. He just wanted to talk about her. "Nothing."

"Are you checking in with your doctor? Or your PT?"

"No, I figure I can handle this recovery all by myself because I have so much experience." His sister made a sound of exasperation. He could practically see her rolling her eyes, too—blue ones like his. In fact, she had all the standard-issue Cartwright features, but on her the square face and strong jaw became uniquely feminine. "Yes, Matty Mom, I have spoken to both of them. I'll be back at Keesler at the end of the month to start my thrilling life behind a desk until I'm cleared to resume training."

"So you're not working with anyone now?"

Jameson frowned. She'd given him the perfect opening. He took the ice off his knee and stood, needing to pace. "Actually, my doctor did send…someone."

"Yeah? Who is this…someone?"

"Did you know Kendra Lonergan in my class?"

"The name is familiar."

"Apparently she works with people who need… Who could use…"

"The word is *help*."

"Something like that." Jameson's imagination supplied a picture of Kendra, kneeling at his feet, massaging his thigh, hands warm and skillful, thick auburn ponytail spilling over one shoulder, green eyes bright with concern. He stifled a groan. Not *that* kind of help.

"Did you know her parents were killed in a car wreck two years ago, days after she graduated college?"

Jameson stopped pacing. It was a few seconds before he could speak. "My God, Matty."

"Mom and Dad told me when it happened. It was all

over the papers in Palos Verdes Estates. Poor kid, it was awful. She has one brother, much older, who lives abroad, I think? Her parents were both only children. Grandparents all gone. She's been alone in the world for two years."

Jameson pushed his hand through his buzzed hair, trying to take in the news. Kendra had been close to her parents. How did he know that? He couldn't remember. His mind was whirling, pressure growing in his chest. He could picture two people. The woman with Kendra's hair, tall and slender, the man not much taller, stocky, both young—his mom's age—with gentle smiling faces.

Kendra. The expert on grief.

No wonder.

"Three months later she went on to graduate school at California State as planned. Got her master's in counseling and started her own business."

Jameson felt a sharp jab of protectiveness. All that on her own, all those months carrying a tremendous load of pain and of responsibility. More than anyone should have to bear, let alone a twenty-two-year-old.

Look at him, whining about how his family drove him crazy. They were alive and they loved him and would be ready to support him again—in their own warped and controlling fashion—whenever he was ready.

No wonder Kendra had looked so ripped open, so vulnerable, when she'd told him about her mom the previous night. Where had she been able to go with her grief? Who had supported her? Instead of collapsing into victimhood, she'd gone out and tried to help others who were suffering.

And he'd been selfishly imprisoned by this place and his poor-me attitude, hiding from the world and the people in it because he had a boo-boo on his knee.

Once again Kendra Lonergan had shamed him. But this time he wasn't going to turn that shame into anger. He was going to use it to help her, too.

"SEE YA." MATTY waved to Joe, one of her favorite cast mates, and stepped out into the twilight of a Sunday evening. The matinee had gone well. She'd felt great about her performance. Without so much worry about Jameson, she had more energy and enthusiasm for everything. She'd even finally had an offer over the weekend on a house that had been a particularly hard sell. Tonight she was going home to leftovers of a really good beef-vegetable soup she and her roommate, Jesse, had made the day before, with rolls from her favorite bakery and an excellent four-year-old cheddar. Plus, the rest of a bottle of the Argentinean Malbec she'd discovered, reasonably priced and delicious.

Life was good! After Jameson had finally answered her call the previous week, she now spoke with him nearly every day; he sounded much more like his old self. Kendra was doing something right.

Which reminded Matty, she'd have to ask what night Kendra wanted to go to the show, so she could—

She sensed Chris an instant before he came into her field of vision, dressed down this evening in a casual shirt and jeans, which he still filled out in all the right places, darn him.

"Good show tonight." Casual, calm, as if there was nothing at all weird—practically outrageous—about him approaching her a second time after she'd told him quite clearly to get lost.

"Are you stalking me?"

He shrugged, watching her intently, like a predator waiting for its prey to strike. "I like the show. You're good in it."

"If it's just about the show, why not go straight home?"

"I think you know the answer to that."

She was afraid she did. Bad enough she'd already had to see him once. But she'd handled that perfectly, cried her few tears, processed their meeting through her system and said a firm goodbye. He'd botched this entrance—his part in her play was over.

"Chris, I don't want to see you anymore."

"You could close your eyes."

She rolled them instead at his absurd joke, an unwelcome smile trying to curve her lips. "Okay. You saw the show, you liked it. I'm really glad. Now I'm going home."

"Would you like to have a drink with me first?"

"*No,* I would not like to have a drink with you first." She lifted her arm and let it slap back down. "What on earth do you think I've been saying?"

"That you've missed me. That there is still something between us and probably always will be."

She scoffed at him. "Those are bad drugs you're taking, Professor. I think you need to lower the dose way down."

"Yeah?"

"Do I even need to answer that?"

He shook his head. "Just have a drink with me. There are things we need to talk about."

"Maybe you do." A couple of chorus members passed close by on their way out. Matty lowered her voice. "I'm happy with how we left things."

"I'm an asshole and you're blameless?"

If the shoe fits. She blew out a breath. "Chris, this was years ago. Years. There is no point bringing it up again. Too much pain, too many accusations, it was all so ugly."

"It doesn't have to be." He took a step closer, voice dropping, a touch of vulnerability in his eyes, not something Chris Hamilton showed often. It could still get to her. *Crap.* "I promised myself I would never look for you, Matty. But also that if I ever saw you again, I would take it as a sign to—"

"G'night, Matty!" Dominique, gossip girl of the cast, peered curiously at Chris, giving him the up-and-down once-over, no doubt absorbing details she could then exaggerate and spread around. A few steps past his sightline, she gave Matty an enthusiastic thumbs-up.

Matty couldn't respond, either to her or to Chris. Why was he doing this? It was so much easier to deal with him when he was being Mr. Smooth. This genuine humility and regret—who could turn her back on that?

Worst of all, Matty *wanted* to talk to him. She wanted the closure she'd never gotten. She wanted to understand why, when things had been crazy, yes, impossible, yes, but so, so good between them in a way she'd never found again, he had wanted to dip his dick into someone as obvious and twisted as Clarisse.

After that, after his thing with Clarisse had fallen through and Matty was long gone, what had he done then? Had he gone through one student after another, trading the old one in when the new one showed up? Or had Matty truly been special and Clarisse some bizarre aberration?

Matty needed to know, even if it hurt. In spite of their age difference, in spite of the improbability of their circumstances, she'd been sure Chris was The One. His betrayal had deeply hurt not only her heart but her faith in herself and in her judgment.

She was relenting, she could tell, and it scared her. Yes, it had been six years, but he could still get to her, and she couldn't afford to lose this battle or herself to him again.

Wait. What the hell was she saying? Matty would only lose herself if she allowed that to happen. She was not a twenty-one-year-old kid anymore, and he was not the man the sun rose and set around. He was the Creepy Professor, as Jameson called him, a man into girls way too young for him.

"Can we go somewhere we can talk?"

"Yes," she answered impulsively, held his gaze, searching for smug triumph—if there was even the tiniest flicker of it, she'd change her mind so fast he'd only feel the breeze of her leaving.

There was none. Only surprise, then relief.

"Thank you." His gratitude, too, was real. "Where do you— I don't know this neighborhood…"

"Green Street Restaurant isn't far. About a ten-minute walk. We can get a drink there."

"Or dinner?"

She narrowed her eyes. "Don't push it."

"I'll try." Chris grinned and reached to straighten the collar of her favorite blue jacket. "It's really good to see you again, Matty."

Matty stepped away from his touch, not sure what to say to that. Because aside from all the lingering anger and hurt he'd managed to unearth, it was really good to see him again, too.

Okay. Now that she'd admitted that thought to herself, she'd suppress it for the rest of time.

Talking rather stiltedly, they headed down El Molino Avenue and turned east on Green Street, heading for Shopper's Way, where Green Street Restaurant, a Pasadena institution, had stood since the late 1970s.

Inside, they found two comfortable chairs at the long wooden bar opposite the low curving wall that cleverly separated tables in one area of the dining room. Behind the bar, windows let in evening light that made bottles and glasses glow in rich shades of green and gold.

Chris pulled out her chair, waited until she was seated before he sat and pulled his chair up next to her. She'd always liked Chris's flair for playing the gentleman—grace and respect, not a hint of condescension. He pulled out her chair because he wanted her to be settled and comfortable, not because he thought she was a dainty flower who couldn't manage the task herself.

"What would you like?"

"Oh." She frowned, mind spinning through possibilities. She hadn't thought past the conversation they were supposed to have. "I guess wine?"

"You're right."

Matty laughed. They'd shared a distaste for women who spoke in questions, something Matty didn't usually do. Clearly she was not in her element. "I would like a glass of wine. Stop. Red, full bodied. Stop."

He put on a pair of narrow-lensed reading glasses, which made him look sexy in the intellectual way she was a complete sucker for, and peered at the wine list. "Looks like mostly California. Here's a gigondas from France, how about that?"

"How can I say no to a gigondas?"

"I have no idea, how can you?" He closed the menu and signaled the bartender, who came right over. Chris had that weird power over bartenders. He was also the kind of guy who could find a parking place in front of a train station at rush hour. Or call a sellout concert and score just-returned tickets. Life seemed to arrange itself to suit him. Kind of sickening, to be honest.

They chatted about the show for a few minutes, an obvious delay tactic that made Matty even more nervous. She was about to break in and demand they get it over with when—thank you, Lord—their wine showed up.

"Cheers." He raised his glass to hers. She nodded, inhaled the rich, complex bouquet and took a polite, experimental sip, wanting to gulp a good quarter of it straight down because in these circumstances she damn well needed it.

"Delicious, Chris."

His mouth broke into a smile of pleasure that took her back six years. The way they'd enjoyed food and wine together had been really special. "Yup. Very good."

"So…"

"You want me to get on with it."

"I do." She put her wine down, determined to drink slowly, keep her wits about her.

"Ah, Mattingly." He sighed heavily. "Okay. Where should I start?"

"How about that night I walked into your place and found Clarisse naked?"

"I already explained…" He held up a hand to stop himself. "Sorry. You want me to do it again."

"Yes." Her throat was already thickening. Damn it, why couldn't she have let this go? Let him go? "I'm better able to listen now."

"Okay." He took another sip of wine, cleared his throat. "Let's see. Clarisse came over—I was just back from the gym—and she came over to my apartment all desperate, saying she needed to talk to me. I'd already heard some about her capacity for melodrama, so I wasn't really worried. I figured she was having trouble in class or something. I let her in, made her some tea, and she suggested that since I was still in workout clothes she could wait while I took a shower."

"Then…"

"Then when I came out of the shower, she screamed. I grabbed a towel, ran into the living room and found her lying naked on the couch, completely fine."

"Mmm-hmm." Matty forced her teeth to unclench. "That part I remember."

"Because you walked in right when I was trying to get her to stand up and put her clothes back on. So it looked like I was…" He gave a short, mirthless laugh. "You know what it looked like."

She bloody well did. The image of him kneeling over Clarisse's naked body, her arms wrapped around his bare shoulders, legs spread wide—that lovely picture hadn't left Matty's brain for…

Okay, it still hadn't left.

Chris's story hadn't changed. And one aspect of it still didn't make sense.

"If nothing happened, why did you let me go?" All pretense at not caring was exposed by her husky whisper.

"Matty." His voice was equally raspy, pain evident in his eyes. "I had nothing to offer you. You were miserable and frustrated. We both were. It seemed the decent thing to do, to cut you loose to find someone else. I was hurt that you didn't trust me, but bottom line, we were in an impossible situation."

"You are right about that."

"I thought you'd come back. Sometime." He stared moodily into his wine. "Then I stoppèd hoping."

No, she hadn't come back. Even after finding out the extent of Clarisse's issues, which meant his story could have been true. Even after Matty graduated and was no longer his student.

"Why didn't you?"

"Because you weren't what I wanted." Matty spoke quietly, but firmly. She hadn't wanted a man eleven years older than she was. She hadn't wanted someone whose class and learning and experience outshone hers by so much. She didn't want a man surrounded daily by young beautiful women who threw themselves at him, whether or not he stayed faithful. And mostly… "I wanted time to discover who I was, apart from the woman my parents wanted me to be. Apart from the woman you wanted me to be."

"When did I want you to be anything but yourself?"

She laughed. "I was twenty-one, Chris. I didn't know who myself was."

He nodded, swirling the rich liquid in his glass. "And now?"

"Now I know."

He raised an eyebrow, devilish and confident again. "You know what that means, Matty?"

"No." She eyed him warily. "But you're going to tell me, aren't you."

"Yup." Grinning now, he reached out and took her hand, drew her fingers between his palms. "It means now is the perfect time for us to try again."

6

KENDRA PULLED HER Lexus into the parking lot north of the Point Vicente Interpretive Center and chose a spot overlooking the ocean. Red-earth cliffs lined this part of the coast, dropping dramatically to a series of coves and beaches for about a dozen miles between Rat Beach to the north and the Port of Los Angeles to the south, where the landscape flattened again.

Jameson sat in the passenger seat; she'd brought him out here for a walk to the whale-watching station. A familiar area, familiar experience, but one that got him out of the house, in ocean air, back with nature. So simple and therapeutic to sit and watch the sea's restless motion, smell the salty fresh air, watch pelicans and seagulls go about the business of living. Most of her clients responded immediately, some with joy, some with hitherto-suppressed tears, some with a release of crippling tension, but very few came away unchanged. She wouldn't risk climbing down to the beach with Jameson today—too many opportunities for knee twisting on the steep, uneven paths—but he'd get plenty from the experience.

"Ready?"

"Sure." He flicked her a glance. Something was different about him today. She hadn't yet figured out what, only that the change made her uneasy.

"Okay." She climbed down from the car—really, she

needed to buy something smaller—and waited for him to come around before they headed toward the path that wound along the sea to the Interpretive Center, which she'd always called "the whale watch place." The Center consisted of a building with a small museum, friendly, helpful staff and a whale-watching station on the outside terrace. December through mid-May during daylight hours, seven days a week, volunteers with binoculars scanned the sea and recorded numbers and types of migrating whales. Farther south, white and proud at the tip of the point, rose the Point Vicente lighthouse.

"So beautiful." Kendra spread her hands to encompass the view and gave a long, blissful sigh. "I couldn't live anywhere else. How about you?"

"For the next twenty years, where I live won't be up to me."

"Twenty." She started walking toward the path that led to the Center, feeling oddly dismayed. "You're staying in that long?"

"That's what Cartwrights have always done."

"After that?"

"Yeah, I'll probably come back here."

She hung back to let a jogger pass, and nearly bumped into Jameson, who'd done the same thing. "What do think you'll want to do then?"

"Oh, probably…circus clown."

"Ah, really."

"Or linebacker for the Packers."

Kendra rolled her eyes. "Uh-huh."

"Then astronaut, most likely."

She snorted. "Okay, smartass."

"All true." Jameson put his hand to his heart. "At least I wanted to be all those things when I was seven."

She glanced at him in surprise. "You weren't born wanting to be a soldier?"

"Airman. Army has soldiers. And no, not me."

"When did that start?"

"Can't really say. Middle school, maybe. When I started clueing into the family history."

Kendra let the silence hang for a few steps, seemingly enjoying the breeze, while she wondered how to phrase her next question. "I guess it would be hard to break a tradition that long."

"Mattingly took care of that."

"Oh, right. She— Mattingly?" She wrinkled her nose. "That's her full name?"

"Uh-huh." He shot her a sideways glance. "We were all named for whiskey. Jameson's Irish, Maker's Mark, Basil Hayden's and Mattingly and Moore."

Kendra laughed, surprised at how comfortable she felt around him today. Sure made a difference when he wasn't snarking at her. "That's hilarious. I never put it together."

"Some do, some don't." He shrugged. "It's Dad's idea of a joke. Where does Kendra come from?"

"Dad's name was Ken. Mom's name was Sandra. They saw Kendra in a baby name book and went 'ooh, perfect!'" She tossed hair from her face, blown there by the stiff breeze, and dug in her pocket for an elastic to control it. "It means knowledgeable."

"Ah, know-it-all, that figures."

"Not what I said." Her hands went through their practiced motions, taming her hair into a ponytail. "What does Jameson mean?"

"Supplanter. When I was little I thought it was something you grew flowers in. I refused to tell anyone."

Kendra giggled, feeling slightly giddy. "What would supplanter mean? Taking someone's place?"

"Yup." He quirked an eyebrow and made quotation marks with his fingers. "Wrongfully or by force."

"Bet you cut in line a lot."

"Nah." His shoulder bumped hers before she could step away. "I think bigger. Maybe a government coup someday."

"Live large, General Cartwright."

"I'm aiming for Colonel by the time I retire."

"Colonel Cartwright has an excellent sound to it."

"Yeah?" He turned his head slowly toward her, grin mischievous, blue eyes warm and alive, utterly transformed from the shut-down guy she'd seen so far into someone boyish and irrepressible. "You grew up fun."

Kendra sucked in a breath. They needed to go on talking. Now. Because she was gazing at him, taking him in, smiling. She hoped she wasn't drooling.

Talk, Kendra.

"My parents used to bring me here a lot when I was a kid." She gestured toward the still-distant lighthouse, aware her voice was too high and silly-chattery. "I used to pretend I knew the names of the whales and their personalities and would tell everyone in earshot all about them, their families, favorite toys, etc. I'm sure the volunteers trying to count them thought it was adorable. And really annoying."

Jameson's smile faded. He put a hand briefly on her shoulder. "I'm so sorry about your parents, Kendra."

Kendra's heart gave an irregular jab. "Thanks."

"I didn't know, when you were talking about your mom, that you lost both of them so suddenly." His voice was deep, sympathetic and absolutely genuine. "Matty told me."

"Ah." Her throat was tight; she stubbed her toe on a rock and nearly stumbled. "Well, thanks."

"It must have been hell."

She could only nod. From the height of giddiness she'd crashed back into grief. Incredible how fast it could happen.

"You have a brother?"

"Mmm." Kendra cleared her throat. "Duncan. He's ten years older. Lives in Wales and herds sheep. We're…different, to put it mildly."

"Did he help out at all?"

She let out a brittle laugh. "Aren't we supposed to be talking about you?"

"Did I sign something saying that?"

"No, but—"

"Did he come home to help you?" There was an odd note in his voice. She struggled to identify it. Not anger, not quite, but almost.

"He came for the service." And left almost immediately after. "He had to get back."

"To his sheep." The disdain was clear enough now.

"No, you don't understand." She tipped her head, eyebrows raised. "He *re-e-eally* likes those sheep."

Jameson cracked up. Kendra's chest loosened. She pointed out toward the spectacular view of Catalina Island. "Look how clear it is today."

He stopped with her, hands on his hips. "How did you manage? Who helped you through all that?"

"Jameson." She laughed awkwardly. "I'm not here to talk about—"

"Did you have uncles? Aunts? Cousins?"

"No. Look, can we—"

"Neighbors?" He swung around to face her, eyes deep with sympathy and something else. "Friends of your parents?"

Kendra turned to keep walking. She could not stand still and stare into those eyes or she'd come apart. "Yes, I had lots of help. Lots of support."

"Uh-huh." He clearly didn't believe her. "Lots. And it was all a piece of cake."

"Chocolate with chocolate frosting."

"So that hell you went through. Alone. That's why you're doing this now for other people. Like me."

"It's definitely part of it, yes." Kendra took a deep breath, trying to regroup. One of the differences between the way she worked with clients and standard talk therapy was that a therapist never—or rarely—brought him or herself into the equation. Whereas Kendra had found that in certain situations, sharing part of her life and experiences could help form stronger bonds of emotional trust. So it should be fine to talk with Jameson about her parents' deaths and her reaction.

It just didn't feel that way.

Immediately her brain started searching for reasons. Because she didn't trust him? Because it felt too vulnerable exposing herself to him? Why?

An answer came surprisingly quickly.

Because Jameson had known her parents, or at least had seen them multiple times, at baseball games and dances and spaghetti dinners and fun fairs. Because in whatever twisted way, he'd been part of her life and her mom and dad's for a long time, and he'd known the three of them as a unit. He was closer to their loss than her clients who were strangers.

Hmm. Not a complete answer, but it was a start.

The path took an abrupt turn to the right after skirting a ravine, and led back close to the sea again. The breeze strengthened as they approached the edge of the cliff, protected by a railing and stern signs warning people not to climb over it. A small flock of brown pelicans rose into view from below the cliff, necks tucked back in flight.

"I guess it must seem strange to you that I'm avoiding my family while you're missing yours."

Kendra shrugged. "Our situations are different, our families are different. I don't judge you."

"You've always judged me."

"Ha! Since when?"

"Since I put worms in your sandwich."

"Um…" She gave him a look, suppressing a giggle. "You thought that wouldn't lead to an opinion?"

"Gosh, no. At least not a negative one."

"Boy logic!" Kendra gave in to laughter. "Hey, I know, I'll ruin her lunch, have people call her 'worm eater' for months and she'll think I'm great!"

"Well?" He sent her a crooked grin. "What's not to love?"

They stopped by the railing to watch the sea heaving in and out, over one hundred feet straight down, wind stiffening now to a good chilly blow. Watching the sea cleared Kendra's mind, the breeze blowing away any lingering sadness.

"Why me?"

"Why you what?"

"Why did you pick on me?"

"Aw, Kendra, why does any kid do stuff like that?"

"Honestly? I can't imagine."

He frowned, shoving his hands into his jeans pockets. "Yeah, good point. For one, you never reacted. It was like nothing bothered you. You were unique."

"So you could get your anger out and not suffer consequences?"

"I wasn't angry with you."

"With your dad. With your brothers." A pair of joggers ran behind them.

"Geez, don't you talk about the weather like a normal person?"

"Nope." Kendra smiled at him, thinking he was like a piggy bank—except for the pink and fat part. If you wanted to get at what was inside him, you'd have to either shake him violently or smash him open. "I talk about you."

"Huh."

"Let's keep walking. Your knee okay?"

"Knee's fine."

Not that he'd admit to pain. She watched him surreptitiously for signs—increased limping, a larger twist to his step, tension in his face. Nothing. Good. She hoped one day he'd tell her if he was overdoing it.

"One time...I don't even remember what I did to you, but I remember your reaction. You looked me straight in the eyes and said, 'People like you feel bad about yourselves, and that's why you need to make other people feel worse.'"

Kendra snorted. "Straight from my parents' mouths."

"It stunned me. I'm serious." He nudged her with his shoulder. "I was supposed to be on the attack, you were supposed to cry. And here you'd flattened me."

"Wait, really?" She turned to see his face, half surprised, half fascinated. "I hurt you?"

His eyes were grave, catching the setting sun, glowing blue. "I have never been with a woman since."

Kendra started to gasp, then, duh, realized he was kidding and burst out laughing. "Stop that."

He grinned. "Maybe one or two."

They approached the Interpretive Center, unstaffed by volunteers at the moment since the whale-watching season hadn't yet started. The light was dimming, sun preparing to sink below the sea. They shouldn't stay long. The park closed at dusk, and she didn't want Jameson walking in darkness in case he stumbled.

Kendra had brought many clients here. With Jameson the view was the same, the lighthouse, the sea, Catalina Island in the distance—all the same, but the place felt different. More as if she was here with a friend, not a client. Odd, since she and Jameson hadn't exactly been buddies. Again, maybe it was their shared history and experiences growing up here.

"Did your parents ever bring you to the Center?"

"Nope." He stared out at the sea, wind making his eyes squint, sexy lines radiating in the corners, the spiky front of his hair ruffling slightly. His jaw was strong, mouth full and serious. Her heart gave a thump.

Yes, Kendra, he is übermasculine and handsome. Get over it.

"Where did they take you?"

"Disney Land. The observatory at Griffith Park. Natural history museum. Baseball games. Basketball games. Los Angeles Air Force Base. March Air Reserve Base. Edwards Air Force Base…"

"No ballet? No symphony? No art or opera?"

"Ha! Uh, no."

"So it was a manly man's upbringing. Where was your sister in all this?"

"Rebelling." He grinned affectionately. "She and Dad were polar opposites."

"Or very similar."

"Maybe that was it. Hey, look." He stepped closer, and pointed out to sea.

"Oh, wow!" Two dolphins, breaking the surface of the water, bounding northward together. The animals gave Kendra a huge charge, no matter how often she saw them. "They always look like they're having so much fun."

"They're free, why wouldn't they be having fun?"

"Free how?" She was so curious about his comment she turned from watching the dolphins to watching him.

"Oh, the questions, Kendra. As Freud is my witness, you do love your questions."

"Don't I?" She blinked sweetly at him. "Free how?"

"Free to be dolphins and do dolphin-y things all day."

"What are Jameson-y things?" She laughed when he started groaning. "How would you fill a day if you could do anything you wanted?"

"Keg of beer and six or seven hot blondes."

"Okay, okay, no more questions. We're done. Let's go home." She turned them back toward the car.

"You hungry?"

His question startled her into hedging. "Not too bad."

"I can make a mean omelet."

"Yeah?" She smiled at him, not that omelets were all that thrilling, but she was still in a smiling mood. "You'll have to show me sometime."

"You busy tonight?"

The wind diminished as the path headed back inland. A beam of sunlight caught him, painting his hair in yellow and rose, throwing shadows and light along his cheekbones, jaw and that sensual mouth. Her heart gave another flip.

Come on, Kendra. Clients had asked to spend extra time with her before if they were lonely. A few had asked her to dinner, and she'd always accepted if she was free. This was completely in the normal range of her treatment.

"I'm not busy." No. She was just confused.

"Good. We can stop at Trader Joe's on the way back and pick up supplies."

"Okay." She walked next to him, feeling rather ludicrously as if she was putting into motion an evening she'd regret. Or as if there was something very wrong with the way she'd accepted his invitation.

It only took her ten more steps and another heart-jumping glance at Jameson's handsome profile to figure it out.

She didn't want to eat dinner with him the way a counselor eats with a client. She wanted to eat dinner with him the way a woman eats with a man.

7

JAMESON STOOD BY the rear of Kendra's Lexus, anxious to get behind the wheel again. His knee was feeling more stable, and he wanted to be in charge of this evening. The idea of inviting Kendra to dinner had been impetuous—the thought of going back alone to the same four walls of Mike's living room had driven him to it—but now that she'd agreed, he was determined to have a fun evening. Show off his cooking skills a little, play some good music, pour some good wine—feel like a normal guy again. Maybe even a normal guy on a date.

If this was her therapy working, she was a genius. But he wasn't sure how much was the therapy and how much was simply being around Kendra. She'd always challenged him, that hadn't changed. But now the challenge was less about proving himself and more about finding out what went on in that beautiful head while she was trying so hard to find out what went on in his. Her reasons might be purely professional—his, not so much.

"Can I drive?"

"Um. Sure." She looked doubtful. "Have you driven yet after the surgery?"

"Oh, yeah, yeah, fifty or sixty times."

"Uh-huh." She tossed him the keys. "Crash my car and I'll hurt you, soldier boy."

"Airman." He caught the keys, feeling better than he

had in…longer than he wanted to think about. "Soldiers, army. Sailors, navy. Marines, marines. In the Air Force we are airmen and airwomen. Get it straight."

"Yes, sir, Lieutenant, *sir.*" She saluted briskly and went around to the passenger side.

He entered the car butt first and swung his right leg over as a static unit, successfully avoiding any twisting of the knee, and therefore any pain. From there the movements required of driving were forward and back, similar to the exercise he did every day. No problem. It felt absurdly good to be doing something as normal as getting from one place to another all on his own.

"Nice car."

"Thanks. It belonged to Mom and Dad. A bit much for me, but I haven't—" She laughed nervously and pulled the elastic out of her ponytail, letting that gorgeous hair fall heavy and free.

"Haven't what?" He started the car, adjusted the seat for his longer legs and the rearview mirror for his height. When she didn't answer, he looked at her questioningly. "Haven't…"

"Been able to sell it." She laughed again, folding her arms and clasping each forearm.

"No one wants this car?" That was hard to believe.

"No, I can't make myself sell it."

"That's understandable." He put the car in Reverse and backed out slowly and carefully, not his usual method. Awareness of his injury made him feel as if he was on the verge of having an accident at any time, even though there was nothing wrong with the car or his driving. Probably the same vulnerability older people felt, and why they drove slowly. "Why didn't you want to tell me that?"

"Because…" She gestured impatiently toward the dashboard. "It's just a *car.* It's silly to hang on to it when I want something different."

"Oh, I see." Jameson nodded as if he'd just deduced something brilliant. "So I'm allowed to have emotions that might not make sense around grief but you're not?"

He came to a stop, waiting to turn onto Palos Verdes Drive, and glanced over to find her with her mouth open, for once unable to come up with a retort. *Gotcha.* She was much too hard on herself.

Kendra closed her mouth, still staring straight ahead. "This is *your* counseling."

"True. It is." He spoke gently, her pain causing him to react with tenderness. Funny how even though he hadn't known Kendra in any real sense at school, being with her now felt as if they'd been friends a long time. He reached over and laid his hand behind her head, intending to give her a quick pat, just a comforting touch. But her hair was soft and thick and felt so good under his fingers that he slid them in deeper, rubbed them gently back and forth over her scalp. "But if I can help you, too, why shouldn't I?"

"Why would you want to?" She turned to him, a combination of challenge and curiosity, vulnerability and strength. Her eyes were large and troubled, her mouth soft, lips slightly parted. His fingers stopped moving. Tightened.

He wanted to kiss her.

Kendra's eyes widened. Had he leaned toward her? Brought her head closer? He couldn't have. How had she guessed?

An impatient honk sounded behind him. Flustered, Jameson started forward, then realized a car was coming and had to jam on the brake, sending a shock wave through his knee.

Ow. Doggone it.

"Uh, sorry." A break in the line of cars opened up and he pulled smoothly into it. "Got a little overeager there."

"Uh, yeah...overeager with the car and something else." She was back, voice vigorous and, yes, challenging.

He chuckled, pleased as hell that she took him on. Though she'd never done anything but... "I have no idea what you mean."

"Just focus on the driving, Lieutenant."

"Yes, ma'am." He turned onto Hawthorne Boulevard, then into the crowded parking lot of the Golden Cove Shopping Center, pulling into a space as close to Trader Joe's as he could, composing a shopping list in his head. He had eggs. Spinach, mushrooms, good bread, greens for salad, a good strong white or a relatively light red, maybe a rioja crianza or a pinot noir. Dessert? In Spain he'd gotten to love the combination of Spanish cheeses paired with quince paste or those incredible soft full-flavored fruit bars he missed.

Marta had been the right woman at the right time, sensual, pleasure seeking—not his forever after, but she sure had taught him about food and wine, about self-indulgence and relaxed in-the-moment living, something he'd never encountered at home. He'd immersed himself in the life until Dad came over and yanked him home. A few months in college with the start of his ROTC training had put him back on the goal-focused Cartwright straight and narrow. But it would be nice to taste those concepts again with Kendra, even for a few weeks.

"Ready?"

"Sure." She strode along next to him. He liked that she was tall, five-seven, he'd guess. He liked that she walked with confidence. She'd always walked that way, as if she was absolutely sure where she wanted to go, leaning forward slightly, feet working to catch up to her body. "What are we buying?"

"Food."

"You want me to eat *that*?"

He grinned, wanting to touch her again, but holding back this time. She seemed as keyed up as he felt. Maybe that moment in the car hadn't belonged only to him.

Inside, he grabbed a basket and headed for the produce section, where he picked out fresh spinach and mushrooms for the omelet, mixed baby lettuces, scallions, cherry tomatoes, a ripe avocado and tiny cucumbers for the salad, then red seedless grapes for cheese, since he wasn't in the mood to go on a long search for quince paste.

"You know what you want." She spoke admiringly.

"In Madrid, refrigerators are tiny. People go to shop much more often than we do here. There are outdoor markets everywhere and everything is in peak condition. Bread is fresh every day. It's something."

"I'd love to go there."

"I'd love to take you." He spoke without thinking, then had to cover himself by winking at her startled expression. "Let's find some cheese."

They wandered over to a case holding an impressive collection from around the world. He picked up a wedge of "drunken goat," a semifirm goat cheese soaked in red wine, and a good piece of manchego, remembering the rich nutty flavors he'd come to love.

"You must have had incredible food experiences in Spain." She was looking at him thoughtfully.

"Why do you say that?"

"Because I've never seen you this animated. Or moving this fast."

He wanted to tell her that his energy had more to do with her than food. "I remember telling my brothers about the cheese and sausage shops in Spain. They looked at me, totally unimpressed, and I realized they were probably imagining shelves of plastic-wrapped orange and white rectangles, and a few sticks of pepperoni. It's nothing like that. This food is practically alive."

"Alive. Wow." She was laughing at him, eyes shining. He didn't care. "You lock your doors at night? In case some crawls in with evil intent?"

"You need to be careful." He took her hand and pulled her, laughing, to the bread aisle, where he looked behind and around him. "We're safe here."

She rolled her eyes and picked out a baguette in a brown paper bag. "For dinner and weapon."

"Good thinking."

He picked out wine next, a garnacha, which would be fine with both the omelet and the cheeses—two bottles for good measure.

"You're in your element." She was smiling at him again in that way that made it seem as if she'd just made an amazing discovery.

"I like to eat good food. I like to drink good wine."

"How's the food in the Air Force?"

"Not Spain, but it's not bad." For the first time he could talk about his experience without feeling that desperate sinking in his stomach. His knee was healing. The pain was receding; he could almost walk normally today. He'd go back to Keesler and get on with his life in the Air Force. He felt sure of it. Maybe at some point he'd even be able to look at another cat. "Don't ask me about the hospital food, though."

"That bad?"

"I was too pissed to taste anything." He stopped by a shelf of chocolate. "Are you a dark or milk woman?"

"Dark."

"I like dark, too." He added a bar, feeling as if they'd shared something significant. Oh, yeah, he had a big old crush. "Let's go check out."

She hurried after him. God, it felt good to be walking at a near-normal pace again—somewhere that wasn't a treadmill. He really had shut himself in. A mistake.

"Hey, Jameson."

"Hey, what?" He picked the shortest line and turned.

Kendra was taking her colorful purse off her shoulder. "I want to make sure you let me pay half of—"

"Nope." He cut her off with a raised hand. "My house. My food. My treat."

"Mike's house, my treatment plan, my—"

"Nuh-uh. You're off the clock."

She blinked, holding a twenty in her hand. "What do you mean?"

"I mean, Ms. Lonergan, tonight you are my dinner guest, not my therapist."

"Counselor, not therapist."

"Counselor. So put the twenty away. If it really bothers you, you can have me over some night to your place."

She blinked again. "But that would be like…"

"What?" He started casually loading their purchases onto the belt. "Like we're dating?"

"No." She shoved the twenty at him insistently. "No, of course not."

"Of course not." He held her gaze with a half smile until she turned red and looked away. Tonight was a date, as far as he was concerned. But if she wasn't comfortable calling it that, he wasn't going to push it. He took the twenty. If it made her feel better about it, fine. He'd use it to buy her something. "Thanks."

"Is that enough?"

"Plenty." He nodded to the cashier, who chatted agreeably about the weather and the wave conditions. Fall was a great time for surfing in Southern California, though between the Air Force and his knee, he wouldn't be on a board again for quite some time.

"You surf?" He took the bags and escorted Kendra out to the rapidly darkening parking lot.

"Not me."

"A non-surfing Southern California girl? What *did* you do as a kid?"

"Oh, let's see. Not much." She started counting on her fingers. "I took flute lessons, ballet lessons until they got to toe shoes and I couldn't stay up on the darn things. Swimming lessons, tap dance, jazz dance, voice lessons..."

"Weren't you ever home?"

"At home I read everything I could get my hands on, did needlework, knitted, made my own clothes."

"Good God, do I need to check you for wiring?"

She blew out a breath as if the recitation had stolen too much of hers. "In short, Jameson, I did anything that involved learning a skill and had nothing to do with socializing or school."

He was laughing, not because she'd said anything funny, just because he was having so much fun with her. "C'mon, you had friends."

"I did have friends. But many of my social interactions in grade school were less than ideal." She sent him a pointed stare. "Though I did write for the school paper."

"The Pen."

"That's the one."

They reached the car, opened the back for their haul. "Did your parents push you to do all that stuff?"

"Oh, no." She shook her head emphatically, making that glorious mane ripple around her pretty face, its color enhanced by the evening light. "That was all stuff I wanted to do."

"You make me feel lazy."

She looked at him with scorn. "Only because you are."

Jameson hadn't laughed this much in weeks. He loved the way she could tease him, totally deadpan, and know he'd get it. He had that kind of connection with Mike. His sister. Not many others. "Can I drive home?"

"You've got the keys." She swung gracefully into the passenger side.

Jameson climbed into the driver's seat—without any grace whatsoever—and started the engine. "Home sweet home."

"You looked up any old friends since you've been back?"

"Nope. But I was thinking this morning of going to see my favorite math teacher ever, Mr. Vinely, at Palos Verdes High. Want to come with me?"

Immediately she started hedging.

He just smiled, letting her be all flustered and stutter out reasons not to spend more nonprofessional time with him, and drove straight to the condo.

The omelet came out perfectly, light, tender, fragrant with mushrooms and a pinch of dried thyme. The bread was beautifully crusty with good flavor, the grapes sweet, the cheeses nicely ripe, complementing the deep, smooth taste of the wine.

They were lingering over that garnacha now, their first glass from the second bottle, seated on Mike's balcony, bundled against the chilly air—Kendra looked incredibly hot and sweet in his Air Force hoodie sweatshirt—admiring the distant view of the ocean.

Most important part of the meal was that cooking it together had been a blast. He'd showed her how to shake the pan, stirring, so the omelet cooked quickly and evenly. She'd rolled it onto a plate herself, only slightly clumsy. They'd laughed and talked more easily, less sparring, more sharing.

He liked being with her. A lot.

And right now, softened with wine, she was absolutely irresistible. Her smile slowed, as did her words. Her body had turned languid and relaxed. Jameson found himself occasionally imagining that body tucked against his in sleep. And tucked against his in...not sleep.

"I think I've had enough." She put her wine down on the small glass-topped table between them. "It's so good, but if I keep drinking I won't be able to drive home."

"You know your body." He bit his tongue to keep from saying he wanted to know it, too, and that he thought her inability to drive home would suit him fine. But maybe it was just as well. She was already making him think about sex. If she stayed longer and he had much more wine, he'd be thinking instead about seduction.

Call him old-fashioned, but he thought it was a lot smarter to decide whether to start a sexual relationship with a woman when he was sober. He hadn't followed that advice once, partying here in town the summer after his sophomore year with a girl he vaguely knew who'd attended a neighboring high school. It had nearly taken a restraining order to get her to stop texting, calling and coming by the house. Dad had been livid. *That's what you get for thinking with your dick.*

Kendra blinked sleepily and stifled a yawn. He wanted to gather her in his arms, put her to bed in Mike's room—assuming he could make himself be that much of a gentleman—and cook her breakfast in the morning. Including a pot of brutally strong coffee.

"This has been great, Jamie—Jameson."

Her use of his nickname startled him pleasantly. Only a few people had ever called him Jamie. His mom, his aunts and Matty. The way it had slipped comfortably out of her mouth, then been immediately corrected, intrigued him. She was feeling closer to him. Fighting it.

"I've had fun, too."

"I should go." She spoke regretfully, then didn't move.

Jameson didn't want her to leave either. But he was more sober than she was.

He stood in front of her chair, offered her a hand. She took it and he pulled her to her feet, deliberately not stepping back so she'd end up close to him, too close for normal social contact. Not close enough for him. "You okay driving?"

"Sure." She peered up at him. "Um. You're standing in my personal space."

"You don't like it?"

"No." She shook her head emphatically, then poked him gently in the chest. "I do."

Oh, man. He was going to get hard in another point-oh-two seconds. "Then why—"

"That's the problem, see. God, I sound drunk. Do I sound drunk?"

"Only a little."

"I knew it." She pulled her hair back into a ponytail in one fist, then let it fall. "I better go home before I do something stupid."

He wanted to ask *like what?* But he knew. They both knew. She was tipsy and he was not about to—

Well, maybe.

"Mmm, smell that?" She closed her eyes as a breeze wafted over them and inhaled rapturously, swaying closer. "Eucalyptus. I love that smell."

He gave in. Her lips tasted like sweet grapes, rich wine and Kendra. He could savor that flavor for hours.

But he wouldn't be able to because Kendra's eyes shot wide open. She backed away, tangled with the chair legs behind her and started tipping. He grabbed her waist and hauled her upright, shocked at her pallor.

"You shouldn't have done that."

"Kissed you or saved you from falling?"

"The first."

"You didn't like it?"

"I…" She frowned, holding a hand to her head. "I said you shouldn't have."

"You didn't answer."

"I don't want to."

"I'll try again." He pulled her full against him this time, felt her mouth opening under his, her lips softening, an extremely effective aphrodisiac—except he didn't need one.

"Jameson." She gasped his name. "We should not be doing this. No, *I* should not be doing this."

"Wait. You shouldn't but it's okay for us to?"

"No. No." She pushed his arms away. "None of it is okay. You don't understand."

"If you say so."

"I do." She put a hand to her throat, looking as if she was trying to calm her breathing.

"Hey." He gathered a handful of hair to tug gently. "You want me to drive you home, lovely and slightly drunk Kendra?"

"No, no, no, I'm fine." She turned and sprawled over the chair. He lunged for her too late; they fell in a tangled heap onto the deck.

"Jameson, your knee!"

"Not hurt. I'm okay." He untangled himself and helped her sit up.

"Thank goodness." She burst into a sudden giggle that almost sounded like a sob. "I guess I'm not that fine after all."

"Trust me, you are quite, *quite* fine." He got to his feet and pulled her up. "But because I am an officer and a gentleman, I will take you home and not lay another finger on you."

"No?" She sounded confused.

"No." He guided her through the sliding doors back into the apartment, which seemed antiseptic and stuffy after the sweet night air. "Unless you want me to?"

"I should go home."

He grinned, noticing she didn't answer him that time either. Okay. He'd drive her home tonight, let her sober up and wake alone in her bed tomorrow morning.

But next time they got together, they were going to take the next step in exploring this powerful chemistry that had been between them since they were kids.

Only this time their interaction would be totally adult.

8

KENDRA DRIED HER face at her bathroom sink and drank yet another glass of water, staring at herself in the mirror. The second he'd kissed her tonight, it had all come back. How had she forgotten? She'd dreamed about Jameson in high school. Sexually.

It was after that awful day their freshman year at Palos Verdes High School, when he'd asked her to the spring dance. He hadn't bothered her for a while, not at all that year, so Kendra had been surprised when he'd walked up to her. She'd immediately gone on guard, ready for whatever crap he tried to dish out.

Except, he'd looked more nervous even than she was, nervousness they'd both tried to cover with defiance. She wondered now if his friends or brothers had forced him into the prank, because he had clearly not been enjoying himself. Not like when he'd put glue in her hair.

He'd asked her harshly, rudely, certainly not in any way she could have taken seriously. On the last word, his voice had cracked, he'd glanced to his left, down at his feet. She'd laughed, asked why she'd want to go *anywhere* with him and stalked off, still laughing. Because as she'd watched his face, seeing the cracks in his bully facade, it had come to her that what her parents had been telling her all along was really true. The only power Jameson Cartwright had over her was power she gave him.

A short-lived victory. Because that night she'd dreamed about him in a way that gave him the same power he had over half the girls in school, including her best friend, Lena.

It was the night of the dance, but the dance was over. She was standing alone on the beach in a new dress. It had been dark, warm, the waves quiet, sand soft. Then Jameson was beside her; she'd felt no fear or surprise. It was as if she'd been expecting him. Barefoot, they'd walked to the water's edge, where he'd turned and kissed her, tumbled her onto the wet sand. His hands had begun an exploration that brought her body alive for him with pleasure that shocked her even in fantasy.

She'd woken in a rush of arousal and adrenaline, hand already between her legs, seeking something she didn't yet understand. Clumsily she'd stroked herself, feeling the desire intensify, thinking of Jameson's kisses, of how his hand had traveled briefly to where hers now lay, leaving a burning trail on her skin.

Her body had seemed to rise up, catch fire, and she'd let out an involuntary cry. The force of that first orgasm had stunned her. For days after she hadn't been able to look at Jameson, hadn't been able to reconcile her dread and their enmity with this new awareness of him and of what her body could do.

How could she have forgotten that watershed moment in her sexual development had been caused by Jameson Cartwright? And yet, if she'd had to choose one memory to bury in her subconscious, that would undoubtedly have been it. Easier than keeping it around to analyze, safer than the risk of finding out she could be on the same puppy-love train as everyone else. Not being attracted to him had been a kind of power, and she wouldn't have wanted to give that up.

Kendra gulped another glass of water, wiped her mouth

and launched herself onto the bed that had belonged to her parents in the room it had taken her a year to move into after they died, even though it was the best room in the house, with huge windows facing the sea and the city, spreading out across the valley to the feet of the Santa Monica Mountains. She lay on her stomach, arms and legs spread wide, relieved her head wasn't spinning, though she was still pretty tipsy.

Jameson Cartwright.

She moved to her side. Her hand slid slowly between her legs. She was already wet.

Jameson.

With a moan of surrender, she rolled to her back, stroking efficiently now—she was no longer fourteen. Her breath stuttered in. She lifted her hips as the pleasure rose, imagining Jameson lying over her, his hard body sculpted to perfection, his penis searching, finding her, pushing inside. She imagined his pleasure, his groans of ecstasy, his mouth and tongue finding hers.

The orgasm came quickly, a fierce burst that stopped her breath, then contractions she panted through, wanting him with her there in bed with a desperation that almost frightened her.

She came down alone, rolled again to her side, pulling up the covers, looking out toward the glittering lights of L.A. for a long, long time, until her mind calmed, her breath slowed, eye blinks becoming more leisurely, body relaxing toward sleep.

Who knew how many hours later, Kendra lifted her head from her soft cotton pillowcase and blinked blearily toward the door of her bedroom. Had she heard the front doorbell?

She stretched under the covers and yawned, peering at the clock. Seven-thirty. Too early for the mailman or a delivery. She must have been dream—

Ding-dong.

Huh? Kendra pushed off the blankets and rolled clumsily out of bed, groaning. Who would show up at this hour without calling first? Too early for deliveries. Someone at the wrong house? There'd been workmen across the street. Maybe a new recruit had come here by mistake?

Padding through the small hallway connecting the master bedroom to the rest of the house, she checked in with herself for hangover symptoms, happy not to feel more than a twinge at her temple. Drinking all that water had been a good idea. She crossed the foyer, opposite the sunken living room with floor-to-ceiling windows like the master bedroom.

Ding-dong.

"Okay, okay." She peered through the front door's peephole and—

Ducked.

Oh, my God.

Jameson. She wasn't dressed, she had morning-after breath and bedhead, plus she'd been masturbating over him last night. What the hell was he doing here?

Okay. She was a professional. Her client needed her. She would simply reforget the memories of that erotic dream, and forget for the first time how he'd taken her in his arms and with the mere touch of his lips sent her spinning into a place of new and exciting feel—

Um. This forgetting thing wasn't working.

She opened the door a crack. Jameson was holding a bag from Bristol Farms, the upscale grocery with a store in neighboring Rolling Hills Estates. He was showered, shaved and dressed in a light gray shirt that made his eyes even more dazzling than usual.

"Hi, Jameson."

"Hungry?" He held up the bag. "I wasn't sure what you

liked, so I brought blueberry muffins, orange-cranberry scones, cinnamon rolls and chocolate croissants."

Her mouth dropped open.

Jameson frowned. "Too much?"

"You brought me breakfast?"

"And coffee. And orange juice. And bananas. And raspberries with a carbon footprint the size of Sasquatch's."

Oh, my gosh. Kendra caught herself before she melted all over the doorstep. No one had ever done anything that sweet for her before. At least no one she was dat—

No. They were not dating.

"I'm not dressed. Or showered. Or…anything."

"So? Not like we're dating, right?"

She rolled her eyes. Yeah, where had she heard that recently?

"Besides, you've seen me that way."

Yes. She had. But that didn't mean she owed him her own stink in return. At the same time, she didn't want him thinking she had some girlie need to be attractive to him.

Even though she did.

"Good point." She opened the door and the screen, smiling bravely, hoping her eyes weren't superpuffy or crusted with anything disgusting. "Good morning. Come in."

"Thanks." He stepped into the foyer, instantly transforming the elegant tiled space to a cozy area he dominated. Was he that big? Or just that magnetic? She had a feeling the answer to both was yes.

"Nice." He looked across the living room, the dining room to the right with its full-length marble-topped dining table and modern crystal chandelier that looked like a dense, square collection of icicles. "Quite a place."

"I grew up here." *Yeah, no kidding, Kendra.*

"Kitchen?"

"Through there." She pointed to the opposite end of the dining room. "I'll just go clean up."

"Take your time." He moved toward the kitchen, but not before giving her a devastating smile that made her breath back up in her lungs.

Yes, she needed to shower, but she needed even more to regroup. Jameson had always gotten to her—remembering the dream proved that even more strongly. But not like this. Last night the way he'd kissed her, even in her rather tipsy state—or maybe *especially* in that state—had positively upended her. Desire, absolutely. Lust, why not. But…then this odd tenderness, and an even odder feeling of inevitability, of rightness, that came from somewhere she didn't understand. An extension of the old-friends feeling she'd had at the whale-watching center, with someone who had never been a friend or a lover.

There was no way she could feel any of those emotions rationally. All her dealings with Jameson in her younger days had been negative and she had barely scratched the surface of knowing him as an adult.

The shower was warm and comforting; she scrubbed quickly, aware of her naked body in a way she did not want to be with the man who'd restarted her sex engines the previous night now at the opposite end of the house, which he'd walked into as if he'd been visiting his whole life.

Worse, she'd had to remind herself he'd never been there, it felt so natural to welcome him inside. God forbid she'd repressed more memories. Maybe they'd gotten married junior year.

She yanked the tap off and dried herself quickly, dragging on jeans and her oldest shirt in a rather unflattering shade of coral that clashed with her hair. No makeup.

There. That was how much she cared about attracting Jameson further.

Ha! She'd show him. And herself.

Okay, then.

Halfway to the bedroom door, she let out a growl of

frustration, tore off the top and replaced it with an emerald-green cotton sweater with a flattering scoop neck.

Fine. She was weak. And vain. And shallow. But at least the jeans were awful. And made her butt look fat. And she had no makeup on, so she was pale and teeny eyed.

Right.

Three steps toward the door, she veered right and stomped into the bathroom for a tiny smudge of eyeliner, a quick swipe of mascara and a brush of blush.

So guess what, she was human. Whatever.

Back toward the door, five steps this time, nearly there, almost...

Damn it.

She whirled around, practically growling, kicked the jeans across the room and dragged on a casual black knit skirt that barely skimmed her knees.

Fine. She thought he was hot and after last night she wanted to look that way, too, okay? So shut up.

She smiled brightly as she entered the kitchen. "Hey. I feel better. Thanks for waiting."

"That was quick. And you really did look fine." He was standing by the doors leading out to the deck, next to the wooden kitchen table on which he'd laid out the appetizing fat- and sugar-loaded carbfest. His eyes traveled over her appreciatively. "You still look fine."

"Thanks!" She was jittery, overcheerful, acting like a teacher facing a classroom of hostile faces on her first day. And wishing she had on the jeans and awful shirt. "Wow, you *really* brought breakfast. What did I do to deserve this?"

He was watching her with a half smile that made her feel as if he could see inside her and understand everything she was feeling, which made her wrap her arms around herself to block him. "I wanted to see you. After last night."

"Oh. Last night." She laughed, which made her sound like an awkward and embarrassed virgin idiot.

"Kendra." His blue eyes softened and warmed. She needed to stop this—whatever it was—before it went a millimeter further. "Last night was—"

"A bad idea." She pointed into his face. "A very bad idea. You're injured, depressed and facing uncertain life circumstances. I'm your counselor, in a position of responsibility for your mental health, and charged with gaining your trust and respect. If we took this relationship into a, um, into a new dimension, then I'd be—"

"Wait, wait, let me get this straight." He was positively smirking now. "You think I'm the vulnerable patient falling for his therapist because—"

"Counselor."

"—falling for his counselor because she's the only person who'll listen to me? The only person who understands me in my most painful and difficult hour?"

"Well...yeah." She gestured toward him. "Aren't I?"

He looked startled, but barely missed a beat. "And if anything physical happens between us you'll be abusing your position of immense power over my psyche?"

"Yes, *exactly*." She nodded eagerly, like her worst student had finally caught on to two plus two. "You are a dainty little blossom of a person and if you so much as kiss my cheek again, I will inadvertently bug-squash your soul."

He was laughing now. She couldn't help it, she joined him, and the shared laughter felt intimate, cathartic and really, really good.

"Okay, soul squasher, let's eat breakfast." He gestured to a chair as if he were the host in her house. She liked that.

"But wait." She paused, her butt halfway to the chair. "We haven't agreed on anything yet."

"Nothing?"

"I mean about us. About what…" She was turning red. She hated that. He flustered her now as much as he had in grade school, but for different reasons. "About how we—"

"Do this?" He leaned forward so fast she didn't see it coming and planted a quick, soft kiss on her mouth. Then he pulled away and sat down as if nothing had happened while she stayed frozen, butt still a foot from her chair, tweety birds circling her head.

Damn it. He had to stop doing that.

More to the point, she had to stop liking it so much.

And him.

Because…

For a brief moment, together with him in her kitchen having breakfast as if they'd spent the night shaking the floors, the reason eluded her.

Because why?

Because he was a client. Because he was a Cartwright. Because he was here for another two and a half weeks and then would go back to a life in the military that did not include her.

Those were all good reasons.

She plunked her butt down, grabbed the glass of juice he'd poured her and drank as if it were a lifesaving serum. Delicious juice. She bit into a blueberry muffin.

"Mmm!"

"Good?" He chose a scone and nodded, his own mouth full. "Mmm."

Good Lord. He even made enjoying a scone sexy. She was going to have to think new thoughts now, because hers involved Jameson making that *mmm* noise for an entirely different reason.

"Thank you for this." She pulled her coffee closer and took off the lid, releasing steam and a dark, rich aroma. "It's really nice of you."

"I want to keep seeing you."

"You—" Kendra froze, coffee in hand, blinking at him stupidly while he took another bite of scone. He wanted to… He was just announcing it like that? That he wanted to date her? And then he could go back to eating calmly while he waited for her answer?

No, no, that wasn't it. Geez. He wanted to keep seeing her professionally. What had she been thinking? Thank God she hadn't responded any other way.

"Sure. I don't have an appointment until later this morning, so right now is fine. What's on your mind?"

Halfway through her speech, he started a slow smile that widened into a sexy grin. By the time she finished, he was chuckling. "Kendra…"

"What is so funny?"

"I want to see you romantically. I want us to go on dates, not counseling sessions."

"Oh." Her face must be turning traffic-light red. But okay, she'd encountered this situation before and knew how to cope. She laid a gentle hand on his forearm, smiling, friendly. "Thank you, Jameson. But I can't go out with one of my clients."

He stood abruptly and hauled her to standing. She got a brief glimpse of his amused face before he was kissing her. Like he meant it.

Apparently he really, *really* meant it.

"Well, guess what? I'm not your client anymore."

Kendra had to try twice to speak, hands braced against his chest. "But we're not finished. And Dr. Kornish hired me to—"

"You're the best there is, Kendra. I'm totally cured."

"Ha!" She tried to push away. But whatever they did to airmen in basic training built muscles much too strong for her to budge. "Not even close."

"Look." He cupped the side of her face, tipped her head up to meet his eyes. "I want you, Kendra. Badly. I don't think I'm alone in those feelings. What kind of successful professional relationship are we going to have if all we want to do is crawl into bed together?"

His gaze and his words combined to shoot hot lightning through her. She couldn't think beyond the mental picture of him making his way, stealthily, naked, into her bed.

"I guess I..." Kendra closed her eyes to gather her thoughts, because it was pretty impossible to do that with his arms around her, her lips still warm from his kisses and his gorgeous blue eyes boring into hers. She'd been trained in how to dissuade an interested client; she'd had to smack down a few men in the past couple of years—gently, of course. The psychologists' code of ethics forbade romantic relationships between a therapist and client until two full years after therapy stopped. But Kendra wasn't a licensed psychologist. Nor was she providing traditional therapy. "I need time to think about this, Jameson."

"Sure." His lips landed, warm and lingering, on her forehead. Even that made her whole body shiver. "Think about it. Take all the time you need."

Kendra bent her head gratefully. "Thank you."

"You done yet?"

She cracked up, lifting her head. "Hey. You didn't used to be this funny in grade school."

"Are you kidding? Worms in your sandwich isn't the height of comedy?"

"Uh..."

Jameson's smile faded. "Guess I didn't have that much to laugh about."

"Oh, come on. You Cartwrights owned the school. Maybe the universe."

"Nah. I was the same wreck everyone else was. Just better at faking it." He stroked back hair from her face. "You kept it real, though. I admired you for that. Which is probably why I kept trying to knock it out of you."

"Boy logic." Kendra shook her head.

He kissed her, sweetly, almost tenderly, and her heart did some melting it absolutely should not be doing. Bad enough she was hot for him, but real feelings…out of bounds entirely.

"I should leave so you can get your day going. But you'll think about it?"

She nodded.

"Good." He backed toward the door. "Dinner tonight?"

"Jameson…"

He held up both hands. "Just asking. I'll call you later."

She saw him to the door, noticing the limp was even better than the day before, replaced by a bit more of his masculine swagger. The surgery had worked. He'd be gone soon, flying off to the rest of his career like Spirit the hawk, healed and released, twenty years before he could retire, during which time he could get shipped just about anywhere.

What was the point? If she was sure their relationship would only be sexual, that would be one thing. But she liked him. And like plus sex equaled only one thing.

Trouble.

She closed the front door and ran back into her bedroom to unplug her cell from its charger, glancing at her watch before she dialed Lena. Her friend would already be at the office, unless there was typical L.A. traffic from hell.

"Hey, Kendra."

"You busy?" Kendra wandered out into the hall. "Not that you're ever not."

"I have a few minutes, what's going on?"

"Jameson."

"Ooh, Cartwright drama. You have my full attention."

"He's… That is, he… Well, he wants to…"

"No way! Really? Oh, my God!"

"Uh…" Kendra stepped down into the living room, past

the antique piano only her mother had played. "I haven't even told you what he wants."

"He's a guy, what else could it be?"

Kendra cracked up. "You are good."

She outlined the situation, how Jameson didn't seem to be quite the jerk they'd thought he was, to put it mildly, and then described all the talks they'd had, the fun they'd had, the transformation he'd undergone from miserable and barely speaking to fun and funny and incredibly sexy. Only she didn't admit that last part.

"You know, Kendra, you will think I'm nuts, but I wondered sometimes if he was always bugging you because he was into you."

"Ha!" Alarms went off all over Kendra's body. "No, no. This is not about *being* into me. This is about *going* into me."

Just saying it was true made her feel better.

Lena giggled. "Geez, what a romantic you aren't. It could be more than that. You don't know."

Kendra gritted her teeth. She'd just gotten rid of the alarm bells. "He's a guy."

"Guys fall in love, too. And what would be wrong with that anyway? He sounds like he's grown up a lot. He's hot. He's available. He has a job."

"He's leaving."

"Oh, Kendra." Lena was quiet for a good ten seconds, which didn't happen often. "He's in the Air Force, he *has* to go. I know it's soon after your parents passed, but their deaths don't mean everyone you love will—"

Forget alarm bells, Kendra was approaching panic. "Love? *Love?* We are talking about a nice healthy boinking here. Period."

"Okay, not love. But not just boinking, girlfriend. Listen to how you told me about him. Not just, 'Wow, Lena, this guy has a package the size of Florida!' You told me how much you love talking to him, how funny he is… There's an emotional component."

Kendra's throat thickened. She did not want to hear this. Especially because it might be true. Okay, it was true. A little. But not out of control. She could still keep it from threatening her sanity.

"I'm just saying what's wrong with dating a guy you're attracted to who is also attracted to you?"

Kendra bit her lip, staring over the top of the olive tree in her backyard that her father had planted for one of his and Mom's anniversaries. Lena made it sound so simple. Was it? Was she just afraid of falling for Jameson? Of losing someone she cared for all over again? It had been two years since her parents died. Sometimes it felt as if she'd been alone forever; sometimes it seemed a blink of an eye. As she told all her clients, there was no right time to move on from a death. Everyone at his or her own pace.

Maybe her strong reaction to Jameson had nothing to do with falling for him but was simply her body and subconscious telling her she was ready now?

"Yeesh, I have to get to a meeting. Call me later and let me know what you're thinking."

"Sure. Thanks, Lena. Bye." Kendra punched off the phone, more confused than ever. If she agreed to date Jameson…

Even the phrase made her want to laugh. Date Jameson Cartwright! Her lifelong nemesis.

But oh, a nemesis with hot blue eyes, a dynamite smile, mouth by Cupid, body by Air Force. She'd have to be crazy not to want to explore all of it.

And she'd have to be crazier to actually do it.

And yet, as Lena pointed out—

But then again…

She rolled her eyes and shoved the phone into her pocket, heading to her bedroom to get ready to go. She had a full day ahead, including a visit to Crystal with Byron. Maybe later she and Byron could invite Jameson for a frolic on the beach in safe daylight.

If she decided the daylight would also turn into night, she'd have officially resigned as his counselor.

Kendra stopped dead on her way to the front door.

Oh, God.

She'd have to call Matty to stop the payments. Matty would want to know why.

Gulp.

She could say Jameson was cured. She could say he refused to see her anymore. She could say he was a hopeless case.

Argh. She couldn't lie and retain any professional credibility, not to mention she couldn't lie to a sister about the condition of a brother she loved and live in her own skin afterward.

Which meant Kendra would have to come up with some way to tell Matty the truth: that she couldn't accept further payment for treating Jameson, because after almost two weeks it had become abundantly clear that she was going to have to screw his brains out.

Then she could sit back while Matty either laughed her ass off at Kendra or sent brothers Hayden and Mark over to kill her.

But first she had to decide…

Kendra sagged in defeat. Who was she kidding? She'd already decided.

9

MATTY OPENED HER eyes. Light was already streaming in through the not-quite-closed blinds over her windows, which gave onto a charming view of puce siding on the house next door. Ooh, baby. Well, anyway, the day looked to be sunny, which was always cheering. She stretched luxuriously in the old sleigh bed she'd slept in since girlhood. Her mother had been thrilled to get rid of it, having wanted to update Matty's old room for years. While the rest of their Palos Verdes Estates house had changed with the times, Matty's room remained a quaint anachronism, filled with dark wood antique pieces she'd pounced on as an adolescent when her father's parents had downsized into a retirement home. Sometimes she thought she'd been born into the wrong time period.

She turned to peer at the brass windup clock on her cherry bedside table. Yes, she had her iPhone across the room for backup, but she loved this clock and refused to part with it, even if it gained a minute now and then. Or two.

Ten o'clock.

Adrenaline burned as her sleepiness cleared enough to register the day and its significance. Wednesday, November 13, two weeks before Thanksgiving, the day she was to have a late dinner with Chris after that evening's show. He was going to be in L.A. anyway, he'd said. How about it?

She'd suggested lunch in order to keep the intimacy of nighttime and the inevitable alcohol consumption from leading them into more temptation than they'd have at midday in a well-lit restaurant, but Chris had to teach. With her show schedule, it was rare she got to share an evening meal with anyone during the week.

Honestly, she wanted to see him so badly that she'd said yes in spite of all the voices cautioning her. At least this time she was going in with her eyes wide open. And if he fooled her twice, then shame on her; Matty wouldn't even try blaming anyone but herself.

Across the room, her phone played the opening lines of Gershwin's "I've Got Beginner's Luck." She threw off the covers, jumped out of bed. She'd never been a morning person, not even a late-morning person, though given that she worked until after 10:00 p.m. most nights, her schedule was skewed compared to most people's. But this morning she was wide awake. Was it Chris?

Kendra! She answered eagerly. Jameson had made amazing progress since she'd been working with him, much more than Matty could have imagined. He was not only taking her calls, he sounded cheerful and funny and... she'd say back to his old self, except that he was more cheerful and funny than she'd ever known him to be. Kendra must be a miracle worker.

"Oh. Uh, hey, Matty."

Matty stiffened. Kendra sounded cautious, wary, no sign of her usual dynamic optimism.

"What's going on? How—" She was going to ask immediately about Jameson. Not polite. "—are you?"

"Good, thanks. I'm doing well. Just fine. Thanks."

This was weird. "How are things going with my little brother?"

Kendra made a strange choking sound. "Great, actually. Really great. He's made amazing progress out of depression and into accepting his injury. Faster than anyone I've seen, given how low he'd sunk."

Whew. Matty fell back onto the bed, gazing up at the iron-and-glass ceiling light she'd also pilfered from her parents' house. "This is great news."

"It is. Definitely. He even seems more sure he'll serve out his time in the Air Force."

Matty grimaced. She'd hoped Jameson's experiences with Kendra would help him come around to some understanding of how much their father and brothers' influence forced his decision to sign up. "Good to hear."

"So, um…there is one change."

Uh-oh. Matty sat up again. Apparently she hadn't imagined the anxious undertone in Kendra's voice. "What's that?"

"I…you won't need to pay me anymore."

She frowned. "So you're done?"

"Not exactly."

"He doesn't want to see you anymore?"

Kendra made that strange choking sound again. "Um, no, actually, he does."

"So, what, he thinks you should *donate* your services?" Matty couldn't imagine.

"Not exactly."

Something weird was going on here. "Why don't you just tell me, Kendra."

"Yes. I should. Sorry. The thing is, he wants to— Well, I guess I do, too, but certain ethical problems…" She made a sound of frustration. "I mean, if we keep getting together, not really professionally—at least on my part. Or no, not his part either. *God,* I'm doing this badly."

Matty gasped and thunked a hand to her chest, aghast and fascinated at the same time. "You're involved with him?"

"No. No. No, not at all." She sighed. "That is, not really. Or I mean, not yet. Not completely."

Matty rose from the bed and went to the window, yanked open the blinds—good morning, puce. Kendra and Jameson. She should have seen this coming. "You want to date my brother?"

"Matty, I have never encountered anything like this in my professional life. I mean, I have, but I wasn't interested."

"I take it you're interested now."

"...Yes."

Matty frowned and paced her room, window to dresser and back. Okay. So this was not the worst thing in the world. As long as her brother didn't get hurt. "Are you serious about him?"

"No, no, no." She answered a little too quickly, but she was obviously nervous as hell. "No point getting serious. He's leaving. We both know that."

Hmm. Window. Dresser. Window. This could actually be really good. For both of them.

"Matty, this is totally unexpected. I'm sort of a mess over it."

Matty relented. She even stopped pacing. "You sound it."

"The thing is, I enjoy him. A lot. And he seems to feel the same way. Maybe it's our shared history, I don't know. We just really have...fun."

"Fun is what he needs."

"Yes, I mean, I have fun with all my clients, but this got...very fun."

A grin started to spread across Matty's face. Well, well. "You know one of the reasons I wanted you to do this so badly is that I thought Jameson would trust you in a way he wouldn't trust a stranger, no matter how capable she was."

"So you don't mind?"

"I'm only worried because he's vulnerable right now."
A snort came over the line. Matty narrowed her eyes. Oh.
Maybe he wasn't that vulnerable. "Does what I think make
a difference?"

The silence went on so long that Matty wanted to giggle. Of course it didn't. Kendra was probably too polite
to say so. What would Jameson say if he heard Matty was
going out with Chris again? Or anyone from college who'd
known about the affair? They'd all want to give her a huge
whap across the common sense. Would that change her
mind? Probably not.

She took pity. "Kendra, when it comes to matters of the
heart, you gotta do what you gotta do. It really shouldn't
surprise me that you two have found something, whatever
it is, however long it lasts. And if it makes my brother
happy, then I'm all for it."

"I'll still be taking care of him. Trying to make sure
he's doing okay."

Shy tenderness had crept into her voice. Ha! She was
crazy about him. Matty relaxed the rest of the way, grinned
wickedly. "He's not so bad after all, huh."

"Not *so* bad, no. Not like he used to be. He hasn't tried
to trip me in the halls." She was silent for a couple of beats.
"But it's less like he's changed fundamentally and more
like he let himself out of some box."

"Ah, the Cartwright container."

"Maybe that's it." She laughed nervously. "Half the time
I think I'm completely crazy even considering this."

"Tell me about it." Matty pulled up the covers on her
bed to neaten them. "I'm thinking of starting up again with
an old boyfriend and feeling the same way."

"It's scary." Kendra inhaled slowly. "But also exciting."

Ew. Matty gave her pillow a thump. She did not want
to hear how exciting her brother was. "Keep me posted,
Kendra. I mean as a friend. If you want to."

"Absolutely. Maybe we could have coffee sometime? I'd love to meet you."

"Why don't you and Jameson come see the show one night this weekend or next week? I promised you tickets."

"I'll check with him." She giggled. "Okay, this is weird."

"Very." Matty would bet everything she owned that Kendra was blushing like crazy right about then. She ended the call and crawled back into bed, turning on her side, hugging the no-longer-neat covers around her. What was that strange power that bound two people together for so many years? Her and Chris, Jameson and Kendra.

When Jameson had been little, the name Kendra had come up over and over. Kendra was smart. Kendra did a great show-and-tell. Kendra was funny in the school play. Kendra was helping organize a food drive. Kendra was running against him for class president.

But every time Matty had tried to talk to Jameson about this Kendra person and a possible friendship, he'd shake his head fiercely and insist she was fat and annoying, words that sounded straight out of their brothers' mouths. So she'd stopped asking, but kept noticing. His victory senior year as class president was the closest he'd ever been to coming clean about his feelings for her.

Matty had been home for the weekend from Pomona when he'd stalked into her room, looking angry and upset. She knew better than to ask, just waited while he roamed around the room, working on her journal entry until he felt like talking. When he did, all he'd said was, "Kendra ran the better campaign."

"Congratulations, you're a Cartwright." Matty hadn't said that the way their dad would.

Jameson had understood the irony. He'd gone on to blurt out how he'd been surrounded by congratulatory friends after the election, and Kendra had made him feel about six inches tall by plowing determinedly through the crowd, congratulating him and walking away. Matty had listened sympathetically, but really, what could she say? If the world was fair, everyone who got ahead would be smarter and harder working and more talented.

Now through a remarkable set of circumstances set in motion by a stray cat, Jameson might finally get his Kendra.

As for herself and Chris, Matty would have to wait to see.

And wait.

And wait—did a day *ever* take this long to pass? She was at the theater half an hour earlier than usual, desperate to escape her apartment and get started on this last block of time before their date. After the show she was out of costume and makeup and into street clothes and her car in record time. The drive to the restaurant would take twenty minutes with no traffic issues.

No traffic issues! She pulled into a public parking lot around the block from the restaurant where they were meeting, the Lazy Ox Canteen, with three minutes to spare. Hurrying across the dark street and down the block, she spotted the glass-fronted entrance and pushed inside.

The place was narrow, bustling, bar on the left, tables in two parallel rows toward the back of the room. Chalkboards on the walls listed the menu options.

It smelled really, really good.

A man rose from a table on her left. She didn't need to look directly at him to know it was Chris. His form was emblazoned so deeply in her memory that even her peripheral vision recognized him in an instant.

She'd planned to be cool, confident, a bit standoffish, all in the name of self-protection, but at the sight of his handsome face and smiling brown eyes all that sensible stuff went out the window and she found herself grinning for all she was worth.

So be it. She'd never been able to fight her feelings for him—what made her hope she could now?

"Hi, Chris." She hugged him quickly, wishing he didn't smell so good and so familiar. It made her want to hold on and inhale. "Thanks for driving out here."

"You had the late commitment. It only made sense." He guided her to their table, pulled out her chair. Matty would never hold it against a guy not to bother with the old-fashioned gesture, but it fit Chris and she enjoyed it. "How did the show go tonight?"

She grimaced, shrugging out of her jacket. "I missed a step toward the end, but otherwise fine."

"Yeah?" He sat opposite her, somehow too close. This was too intense, too awkward; there was too much unsaid hanging between them to relax. She needed a drink. Now. "What happened there?"

Matty pretended to be very involved in adjusting her chair, using it as an excuse to back up just a bit. She'd been thinking of him. Of tonight. Of what might happen after dinner and whether she wanted it to or not. "Mind-body glitch. It happens. My concentration slipped."

"I couldn't keep my mind on anything but you today either."

He spoke offhandedly, as if he'd been praising the restaurant decor. Arousal burned through her. It had always been like this between them. "What makes you think I was thinking of you?"

"Weren't you?"

She smiled and picked up the menu. "Don't let it go to your head."

"Trust me, with you I take nothing for granted." Chris leaned forward as if to whisper, raising his eyebrows. "Any chance you're in the mood for champagne?"

A joke between them. She was *always* in the mood for

champagne. "Hmm. Well…I *guess* so. Are we celebrating?"

"Just drinking champagne."

"I approve."

They spent a few minutes looking over the menu of small plates, discussing which ones to try—difficult choices, since everything looked delicious. They'd just settled on a couple of intriguing vegetable plates and a few heartier selections of meat and fish when the waiter came by with champagne, which Chris had apparently ordered before her arrival.

Matty scowled teasingly. "I thought you took nothing about me for granted."

"Only this." He smiled at her, eyes warm. "You never say no to champagne."

"True." And she never said no to sex after she'd been drinking it. He probably remembered that, too.

After the waiter filled their glasses and took their order, Chris raised his flute to her in a toast. "Here's to stumbling over you again, Matty."

She hesitated, then clinked his glass and drank. The champagne was chilled just right, with a fresh clarity that slid down way too easily. Matty took in a blissful breath. "Oh, that's good. I'll end up taking a cab home."

"I can drive you." He suddenly looked uncomfortable, lined up his fork more exactly perpendicular to the table's edge. "If it comes to that."

Matty dropped her gaze, took another big sip of the wine, knowing they were both thinking about him coming home with her and what might happen there.

"Catch me up on the years, Chris. Still renting the same apartment?"

He shook his head. "I bought a house when I got tenure. Nice three-bedroom on Seventh Street. I have room for my office, and a guest room. I like the space."

"Still got the baseball wall in your bedroom?"

"Absolutely."

She sipped more champagne, watching him over the rim, feeling the bubbles cavorting through her system. He was so, so handsome. She remembered lying in his bed after they'd made love, staring at the autographed poster of Graig Nettles on the wall and wondering if they'd get married, have kids, be together until death.

So young. So naive.

"Did you ever go to Paris, Chris?"

The warmth in his eyes faded to wistful sadness. "No."

"No?" She was dismayed to find herself relieved. They'd planned to take the trip together after Matty's graduation. Matty had been ecstatic. She'd spent her year abroad after high school in London, Scotland and Ireland, but had never made it to the Continent. Paris would belong to her and to Chris. She'd even fantasized that he'd propose there. After they'd broken up, she'd barely been able to think about France, let alone plan to go there without him. Later there had been other more practical reasons of budget and time.

But *he* hadn't gone? Not ever?

"Why not?"

He chuckled dryly. "Paris was supposed to be ours, remember?"

"But it's been *years,* Chris." Emboldened by the champagne, she laid her fingers on the table, their tips just touching his sleeve. "Why didn't you go later? It was your dream destination."

"Mattingly..." Chris put down his champagne and took her hand, eyes filling with a special sweetness, a look she remembered getting many, many times, a look that made her feel adored and desired and as though the world was a uniformly fabulous place—despite all evidence to the contrary. "I don't think you realize how serious I was about you."

She opened her mouth to scoff at him, but couldn't make a sound. How could she know if he was telling the truth or setting the stage for seduction that would ultimately lead to more heartbreak?

"I know that's not what you want to hear right now, so that's all I'll say." He released her hand and sat back. "Did you ever go?"

"No." She developed the same fascination with silverware he'd had not long before, heart still pounding. "Either I didn't have the money or it wasn't the right time."

"Nothing to do with me, huh."

She grinned apologetically. "I put everything I had into getting over you, Chris. After that it was just lack of opportunity."

"I understand."

Waitstaff began arriving at their table, which was soon covered with plates holding small portions of the most amazing-looking food. They tasted everything, exclaimed over one dish, held out bites of another to try, and soon they'd relaxed into conversation involving the growth of Matty's performing career, getting her real estate license, Jameson's recovery, Kendra and the phone call that morning. Then on to Chris, his hopes and victory over the tenure process and changes in the Pomona faculty and administration and in the town of Claremont.

By that time, their food had been happily eaten, the champagne drained, then quick cups of coffee, decaf for her, espresso for him. The restaurant was closing and it was time to go.

"You okay to drive home?" He took her arm and led her out onto the sidewalk. "Where are you parked?"

"In the lot around the corner. How about you? You have a much longer drive. You're not going to fall asleep?"

"Not me." He squeezed her hand. "I'm wide awake. And not just because of the coffee."

"My show schedule has turned me into a night owl." She wasn't going to admit being with Chris still made her giddy.

"When can I see you again?"

"Soon as you turn your head."

He snorted and pulled her close, put his arm around her shoulders. They still fit together perfectly, their steps automatically syncing. "I've missed you, Matty."

She said nothing, didn't think it wise to push the conversation in that direction now, not when they were both tipsy, it was late at night and they were still under the pull of this remarkable reunion. She needed distance and sobriety to analyze the evening with any objectivity.

They crossed into the parking lot, and Matty felt her tension rising. Good night was coming. God give her strength if he tried to kiss her...

"Where's your car?"

"Um...there." She pointed to the far end of the lot.

"Mine's here." He gestured to their right. "I'll walk you to yours."

"You don't have to—"

"I know I don't have to." He walked with her, humming in his rich, deep voice a tune she vaguely recognized, but couldn't place. As they approached her car, Matty's nerves started humming louder than he was.

He'd try to kiss her, of course he would. Would she have the courage to stop him?

With her body so close, absorbing his warmth, memories of what that body had done with hers clouding her mind, she suddenly wasn't so sure.

They reached her car. She turned to thank him for the evening, telling herself to give him a quick hug and retreat to safety. He drew her into his arms and began a slow waltz. Her mind suddenly supplied lyrics to his humming.

Oh, no. She *loved* that song. So tender, sweet and romantic, it was nearly gross.

"Why are you singing that?"

"No idea." He spun her and brought her back to his arms. "It showed up in my head. What is it?"

"'I'd Fall in Love Tonight.'"

"Were they playing it at the restaurant?"

She laughed, losing the battle to keep at least four inches between them. He was such a good dancer. "Hardly. It's from a hundred years ago."

"Then it suits me. What are the words? I can't remember."

"I don't know them."

"Come on." He kept dancing, humming when he wasn't speaking. "You know the words to every song ever written. Tell me."

She took a deep breath, aware of his arm curving around her back, the warm clasp of his fingers, the way their bodies moved so perfectly together. "It's about the singer touching a lover and having it feel like the first time all over again, and really right. Then the singer says if he or she didn't already love the other person, he or she would definitely fall in love with him or her on that night."

"Uh, Matty?" He stopped, holding her an inch away, looking at her with sexy amusement. "What's that, the legalese version?"

She opened her eyes innocently wide. "It was a factual and succinct summary. Highly appropriate to the occasion."

"I see." He went back to dancing, resting his cheek on her hair. "So you didn't want to stand in my arms in the dark and recite a love poem."

"Not really." She was barely able to make sound. "Given our history."

"I really liked parts of our history." He slid his arm all

the way around her until their bodies were touching. "It's probably why my subconscious came up with that song."

"Possibly. But I don't think—"

His head dipped. His lips found hers. Lightly, gently, he tasted her, smelling clean, masculine and so, so familiar. Her body responded as if it was finally where it belonged.

Another kiss, deeper; his embrace tightened. She'd forgotten his strength, forgotten how she could feel so cherished and so safe in those arms. But she hadn't forgotten what his kisses did to her, how no other man had been able to make her feel so much with so little.

She moaned, pressed herself against him, relief she didn't understand flooding her body, a huge release of some tension she'd been holding since she'd finally walked away from him six years before.

He pulled back, pressed her head to his shoulder and rocked her side to side without speaking. Tears sprang in her eyes; her throat thickened.

Chris.

"I'd like to see you again."

"Yes," she whispered.

"Soon?"

"Yes."

He unwound her arms from his neck, kissed her again and stepped back.

She blinked at him uncomprehendingly. Her body was screaming for his, naked and sweaty, tangling up sheets, rocking sofas, overturning chairs—what hadn't they done?

"The only thing I want more than tonight with you is more tonights with you, Matty. A lot more. If I ask to come over now, we'll be going too fast. For both of us. I don't want to crash and burn again. I know you don't either."

Matty nodded mutely, holding back tears as hard as she could. He was doing the right thing for the right reasons. Someday they'd have to talk more about Clarisse.

He'd need to go over it again. And maybe again after that, until she trusted he was telling the truth. But he was right, they needed to rebuild that trust slowly after it had been so thoroughly smashed the first time.

She got into her car, feeling a different kind of relief, this time mixed with longing and wistful regret. "Good night, Chris."

"Call or text me when you get home."

She smiled. Chris had always insisted. Even if she was just walking the few blocks back to her dorm. "I will."

"Sweet dreams." He tapped on the door and stepped back. She backed out of the space and drove off, waving, glancing at him occasionally in her rearview mirror.

Just before she lost sight of him, he tipped an imaginary hat.

10

JAMESON LEANED HIS elbows back on the ancient quilt he and Kendra had spread on Rat Beach—so named not because of rodents, but because it was the beach Right After Torrance. The day was chilly but the sun was warm, and as always the beach was not at all crowded. Frankly, if he could lie next to Kendra on a blanket he would do so even in Antarctica. She was leaning back in the same position he was, her hair a thick curtain between her head and the quilt, making him want to put his hands into it, feel it spreading across his chest...

She'd picked him up after her last appointment and they'd gotten takeout and brought Byron to the beach. They'd been chatting pretty easily during dinner, but there was still underlying tension. There probably would be until they settled into the rules of phase three of the Kendra-Jameson relationship—from grade school enemies to counselor and client to...whatever this was going to be.

Jameson was hanging back until he found out. The chemistry between them had made it pretty obvious maintaining a professional relationship wasn't going to work. He couldn't see her without wanting to touch her, kiss her and...yeah, um, a lot more than that. Hell, he felt that way about her even when she was out of sight.

But this was more than a simple working out of male-female urges. He liked Kendra a lot. He respected her. He wanted to find out more about her life since high school, how she'd weathered the tragedy of losing her parents and what she wanted for her life in the future—whether that could involve a long-distance relationship. And lately he'd found himself wanting to protect her. To keep her safe from the big bad guys of life. To be the one she turned to for advice and support.

Not great ingredients for a casual two-week fling. Yet the thought of ending whatever this turned out to be was nearly as ridiculous as thinking about waiting twenty years to live with her again in the same town.

Behind them Byron let out an impatient woof. Kendra groaned and dragged herself to sitting. "I should let him run around. Why didn't you stop me after I'd eaten enough for three people?"

"I was too busy eating for seven." Jameson surveyed the wreckage strewn around them. Thai food. Decimated. The battle had been long and delicious, starting with tom yum kai soup, a spicy flavorful broth brimming with shrimp, straw mushrooms and cilantro; then fiery, rich red curry with beef; and finally pad thai, rice noodles slightly sour from tamarind juice, rich with peanuts and egg and refreshed with lime and bean sprouts.

"C'mon, Byron." She got to her feet and untied his leash, then headed for a corner of the quilt. "I have a present for you, Jameson. Want it now?"

"A present?" He pretended childlike eagerness. "Where? What is it?"

"Here. Wait." She reached into her bag and came up with an old chewed-up dog toy.

"Ooh, slobbery tennis ball, thank you!" He grinned at the look she sent him.

"That would be for Byron. This…" She pulled out a sketch pad and a variety of pens, pencils and charcoal.

"...is for you. While I let Byron go nuts off leash, you go nuts on paper."

"Kendra. Wow. Thank you." He took the art supplies from her, admiring the thick sheets of paper, the sharpened high-quality drawing implements. She must have made a special trip to an art store to buy them for him. More touched than he should be, he pretended sudden suspicion. "Wait, this is therapy. I thought you weren't treating me anymore."

She stood with Byron's leash, making the dog shoot to his feet, wiggling all over with excited anticipation. "You don't think friends should help each other?"

Friends? Was that what she'd decided they were? He couldn't blame her, given that he had nothing to offer her but the next two weeks. Yet he couldn't help a sharp jab of disappointment. "I don't want you to do your job and not get paid."

"Oh, yeah? Well, I want you to draw me something." She staggered as Byron pulled in the direction of the water. "Then I think we need to take a long walk and burn off one or two of the sixty thousand calories we just ate. If your knee is up to it."

"Absolutely." His knee had been improving rapidly. Sometimes he wondered if Kendra had affected its recovery as positively as she'd affected his attitude. He only had minor pain now, though he was still careful and did his home exercises diligently, lengthening his stationary bike and treadmill sessions gradually and sensibly, even while his body was yelling at him to push to the limit or he'd fall behind.

But Dr. Kornish had told him horror stories about doing too much too soon. No, thanks.

Speaking of Dr. Kornish, his nurse had called that morning to check on Jameson's progress. When Jameson had praised the work Kendra had done on Dr. Kornish's behalf, the nurse had had no idea what he was talking about.

Smiling, he watched Kendra unhook Byron's leash and race with him down to the water. A sweetness came over him that he hadn't felt in way too many years. Self-consciously, he flipped up the cover of the sketch pad, still squinting at woman and dog and water. Jameson hadn't put pencil to paper since college when he'd designed a publicity poster for a friend's variety show. However, his incredibly sexy ex-counselor "friend," whom he desperately wanted as a lover, had requested he draw for her, so he would.

He let his gaze focus, wander, allowing his artistic eye to take over. Cliffs, palm trees, ocean, surfers and an auburn-haired laughing beauty, legs long, body slender, strong arm throwing a tennis ball into the waves for a crazed canine over and over.

His pencil moved swiftly, a few lines for her torso, the curve of her back, catching her bending to the dog in welcome, skirt blowing in the breeze, hair streaming behind her. Horizon, sea, sky—the page went up and over. Again he drew, this time capturing her larger center frame, stretched in the act of throwing, her body a graceful arc, texture for her hair, her clothes. Up and over. Then again, the strong breadth of her shoulders, the contour of her breasts, the sensual flare of her hips. Up and over. Her head in profile, full mouth stretched in a smile, faintly freckled straight nose ending in a sweet point, cheekbone shaded high, long-lashed eye suggesting joy, brow an expressive slash, hair spilling back in a generous tangle.

She was beautiful. He must have noticed in high school. Beyond the few extra pounds, the heavy dark glasses, the serious demeanor. He must have seen her, internalized her features. How else would he be able to draw this face from memory so easily?

"Can I see?"

Jameson started and hid the drawing instinctively. He hadn't seen or heard her approach. "Not yet."

"You okay for a few more minutes? I want to put Byron in the car."

"Sure."

He watched her walk, hips twisting saucily to gain traction in the sand. His fingers itched to draw her again.

Up and over.

This time he embarked on a full portrait, working the details of a more distant memory. Kendra, cheeks and chin fuller, brows thicker, mouth a line of determination and strength, eyes direct and assessing behind black plastic.

The face he'd encountered many times, most recently after he'd stolen the election from her their senior year. He'd never forget it or how she'd made him feel that day.

A few more details, hair, then the plain collar of a gray shirt.

He glanced over to see her coming back already, down the steep hill from the school parking lot up top. There was no hiding from her. She drew the best from him, goaded him to be his best self. Then and now.

How could he not be falling for her?

She was striding toward him, her smile reaching out. Jameson put away the pad, his instinct to stride over to meet her, scoop her up in his arms and bring her back to the quilt to make love to her. "Can I see now?"

"Later." There was too much of himself and his feeling in the drawings. He wasn't ready to share that yet. "After the walk."

She narrowed her eyes. "Stalling, stalling."

"Can if I want to."

Her giggle at his childish chant made his day. He helped her pack up their leavings, then got to his feet, stretching his right leg, flexing it carefully. His knee still became unwieldy when it had been quiet for too long, but his range of motion was nearly back to normal.

In two weeks plus he'd be back on base. Another three to six months before he could hope to restart his specialty training program, depending on his physical performance and what openings they had for him. He wasn't panicking quite the same way as he used to at the delay. He could probably credit Kendra with that, too.

Trash cleaned up, shoes left behind, they headed bare-foot toward the water where the packed sand would make walking easier, then north toward Torrance Beach and the start of the South Bay bike trail, which he used to ride round-trip all the way to Santa Monica, slightly over twenty miles each way. Stunning ride. He'd like to do it with Kendra someday.

Someday. In the brief pockets of time when he'd be back over the next twenty years? They wouldn't have the chance for a someday.

He grabbed her hand because he had to touch her, hold part of her as if to keep her with him. She was so beautiful striding next to him, legs swinging freely over the packed sand, hair flowing out behind her, green eyes catching the rays of the setting sun. Her cheeks were flushed pink and her skin looked so smooth and soft his lips ached for it. "I had an interesting phone call today."

"Yeah? One of your Air Force buddies?"

"Dr. Kornish's office."

"Uh-oh." Her eyes darkened in concern. "What was that about?"

"Just checking on me. Everything seems fine. I thanked his nurse for the fabulous treatment I'm getting from a Ms. Kendra Lonergan they'd never heard of."

"Oh." Her lips twisted. She sent him a sideways look. "How about that."

"Yeah, how about that?"

She wrinkled her freckled nose, looking absolutely adorable but not horribly alarmed, not as though she'd told a horrendous lie and was about to be seriously busted. "I guess I should confess, huh."

"Might be a good plan."

"I'm an impostor, Jameson." She threw up her hands in mock despair. "A fake, a phony, a fraud."

He tsk-tsked, enjoying her melodrama. "How bad is it?"

"I'm really a grief counselor. I really have a practice in Palos Verdes Estates and beyond. I really do work in conjunction with therapists and many doctors. Just not Dr. Kornish. Or the Air Force."

"Who sent you?"

"Does it matter?"

A lightbulb went off. He made a sound of exasperation. Who else would know and care enough to meddle? "Okay, which one?"

She looked at him in confusion. "Which one what?"

"Mom, Dad, Hayden, Mark or Matty?"

"Ah." Her face turned prim but he saw her lips twitch. "Unfortunately, I am not at liberty to disclose the identity of the— Oh!"

He swung her around, pulled her into his arms and kissed her, hard and full on the mouth, dipping her back so she clutched his arm, afraid of falling.

She gasped when he pulled back. "What are you doing?"

"Kissing you." He did so again, longer and sweeter this time, because as always once was not nearly enough.

"I know that, but—"

Twice wasn't enough either. Her mouth was enticing, lips soft and responsive. His body reacted to their touch as if she'd been naked, performing an erotic dance on top of him. What would it be like to make love to her? He probably wouldn't survive the experience. But he'd really, really like to try.

"*Now* are you ready to confess, Ms. Lonergan?"

"I'll never talk. No matter how much you torture me." She lifted her chin in defiance. "Though...you can keep trying."

He grinned and let her stand straight, fitted her body full against his so she'd feel how much he wanted her. She gave a tiny whimper and pressed against his erection, nearly causing him to lose his mind.

Kissing was not going to be enough for long. He bent his forehead to hers and fought down the lust response. Public beach. Stopping was a good idea before he was tempted to take her right here and get them both arrested. And sandy. He took her hand again to continue their walk, making a mental note to turn back soon. To take her back to his place, her place, any place that had a bedroom. And a bed.

He imagined her naked, that glorious hair spread out around her, around them both, and gave a silent groan.

"You okay? Is it your knee?"

"No, no, I'm fine." Oops. Apparently not a silent groan. What had they been talking about? "So some Cartwright committed the mortal sin of wanting to help me."

Kendra pressed her lips together, which pouted them out slightly and made him want to taste them again. "Certainly possible."

"And he or she figured I'd be about as welcoming as a bear woken from hibernation if I knew a family member sent you."

She knitted her brows, sent him a sidelong look. "That is a logical supposition."

"And so this Cartwright decided you should tell me this was an Air Force doctor–led program so that I'd feel I had no choice but to put up with you."

"Well, Jameson." She tapped a thoughtful finger to her lips. "I suppose that would make sense in the abstract, but of course I can't really say."

He shook his head, grinning, and pulled her closer in order to bump her away again with his hip. "It's devious, untruthful and yes, I suppose given the circumstances it makes sense."

"It does. I mean, imagine me showing up when you were so down and miserable and saying, hey, I know! Let's do some counseling! Really, it'll be fun!"

He made a face. "I see your point."

"You were *so* down, and *so* disgusting to be around and so-o-o—"

"Uh, yeah. Right. I get it." He glared at her, dropped her hand then pulled her closer, arm around her waist. "What convinced you to help me?"

"The money."

He forced a laugh, annoyed at himself. What, he'd expected her to say, *Oh, Jameson, you know how you've always been special to me!*

Actually, that would have been great. "Money, huh?"

"It's all I live for." She nudged to show she was teasing. "Really, I was curious. I wanted to see the great and powerful Jameson Cartwright brought low."

"By a cat."

She smiled, eyes sparking mischief, skirt swirling enticingly just above her knees. "You know, that's the first time you've been able to mention that species."

He faked a shudder. "Evil creatures. Demon spawn."

"Have you always felt that way?"

"Nah. I like cats. *Used* to like cats."

They walked on. He sensed her withdrawing into thought, surprised at how easily he could read her moods and body language.

"Actually." She was looking down now, concentrating on the flat sand under her feet. "I've been thinking of getting a dog for a while. Though I hate to give up working with Byron."

"Why don't you get one?"

"I don't know." She frowned as the incoming tide brought a wave close to her toes. "Sometimes…I'm afraid it's because I'm scared."

"Of dogs?" He knew that wasn't the answer, spoke gently to encourage her. Her struggle to confide in him made him want to put his arms around her and make her whole world safe. Twenty years. Damn it.

"Of losing one."

Jameson took time to process that, slowing as the next wave led a mighty charge and sloshed cold water over their feet. She couldn't bear to fall in love with a pet only to have it leave her. Like her parents had left. Like Jameson would, in two weeks.

A frisson of panic climbed his spine. There wasn't enough time. Not enough to get serious. Not enough to lay any claim to Kendra after he was gone. She'd be free to meet someone else when she was ready. Fall in love. Have kids.

The thought was eating him up, and he'd done nothing more than kiss her.

But then, he hadn't been able to think calmly about Kendra Lonergan since he was six years old.

"Give yourself more time. You'll be able to love again someday. Look how your whole life is structured around caring for people. It's in your nature."

"Yes. But I would like to be able to do it now." She sounded vulnerable, shy, totally unlike the Kendra he knew.

"Maybe you can."

"Jameson…"

He reacted on pure instinct, reached for her and locked her in his arms, held her tightly, cold water swirling around their feet, splashing up on their lower legs, pulling at their ankles as it retreated, leaving bubbling patterns in the water and rivulets in the sand.

This time their kiss was different. He wasn't sure how at first, only that it wiped his brain clean, dwindled the world to the two of them and their mouths, their breath, the moisture on their lips and a powerful connection that sprang to life.

Awed—nearly overwhelmed—he pulled back. For a second before she masked it, he saw the same fear and vulnerability on Kendra's face that he'd heard in her voice.

"We're talking about a dog, right?" Her eyes were serious on his.

"Of *course* a dog." He kept his gaze on her, equally serious. "What else would we be talking about?"

The ghost of a smile curved her delicious mouth. "No idea."

He leaned down, rested his forehead on hers again. "Would you like to come over to Mike's place, Kendra?"

"I was going to invite you to mine," she whispered. "I need to take Byron back to Lena's. It's only a few blocks away."

"I'd like that." He straightened, trailed fingers down the side of her face, then turned and walked with her back toward their quilt, thinking about the night to come.

And it occurred to him in a rush of certainty that he'd been in love with Kendra Lonergan his whole life. And that he had only two weeks to prove to her she could love again—and that she'd always belonged with him.

11

THEY DROPPED BYRON off with Lena, who greeted Jameson warmly, chatted cordially and, every time his back was turned, made lewd tongue-hanging-out faces at Kendra, who could barely keep a straight face. Yes, Lena, he was hot. A large part of the reason she'd decided spending tonight together was a good idea. For both of them. Both were in need of human contact and tenderness, and neither would risk much. He had a foot in the military and she'd discovered her parents' deaths had left her with a reinforced steel wall around her heart to keep her from feeling too much. Funny how she hadn't realized it was there for so long. A certain numbness after the initial agony of grief subsided was normal. But she hadn't understood how effectively hers was working until it had faltered.

She loved the way Jameson was so playful and teasing and affectionate. When he'd introduced kissing into their friendship, she'd taken it as a flirting extension of the same. But an hour ago, during their walk on Rat Beach, after she'd been talking about her fears, a friend-to-friend confession, he'd kissed her differently. In response part of her wall had softened. Only a part, only for a short time.

But for that moment she realized how long it had been since she'd allowed herself to feel her own emotions. She'd become so used to—and so skilled at—repressing them in order to concentrate on her studies, and then, in her career, on the feelings of others, that she'd neglected herself.

So many things now made sense. Why she hadn't moved out of Mom and Dad's house. Why she hadn't traded the car, bought a dog, left the area even for a short time—so many steps that would define a true end to her childhood and to her life as a daughter. Steps that would symbolize the embracing of her life as an adult woman. Alone.

All very deep thoughts, ones that would require more analysis and decisions, but as she pulled into her driveway, she decided that serious thoughts could damn well wait, because she was only about twenty yards from her bedroom and beside her was a guy she'd come to like a whole lot, and trust, and feel comfortable with—about as differently as she'd felt about him in high school as you could get.

As long as she made tonight about an extension of the playful fun between them, she'd be safe.

"Home sweet home." She turned off the motor and smiled sweetly at Jameson as if she wasn't planning to have him naked as soon as was decent after they got inside. She figured three or four seconds would do it.

"Nice to be here." Jameson threw her a sexy sideways look as he opened the door. They were going to have fun tonight.

He joined her on the short walk to the house, which was taking forever.

"Lena seems great. I didn't know her in school."

"She's as good as it gets." Kendra's keys were already out. "I would probably have lost my mind over the last couple of years without her."

"Then I like her even more."

The front door was open. They were inside.

Three…two…one…

No! Not yet.

"Would you like a drink?" She tossed her keys nonchalantly onto the table by the door, pretending she hadn't just had a near panic attack.

"Sure. If you're having one."

"I think I will." She strode toward the kitchen, aware of him following closely, wanting to turn and kiss him, but also…not. "Beer? Wine? Something stronger? Whiskey in honor of your father?"

"Got any bourbon?"

"We do. That is, I do." She opened the cabinet that her father had kept well stocked. He and Mom hadn't been big drinkers, but they'd liked their little sips every night, and they'd liked to be able to offer guests whatever they wanted. "Let's see. Maker's Mark, named after your brother, Old Grand-Dad, fortunately not named after your brother and Woodford Reserve."

"Woodford. Excellent whiskey. Thank you. Are you having some, too?"

"Absolutely." She took down the bottle, thinking she could use about a gallon. That kiss on the beach must have unsettled her more than she'd thought. Or maybe she was just nervous because it had been a while since she'd slept with a man. Not that she'd forgotten how.

She assumed.

The last guy she'd been with had been her year-older boyfriend in college, Grant, who'd decided he had to go on to law school unencumbered by anything as distracting as a woman in his life. Last she'd heard he'd flunked out because of too much partying.

Yeah, because that wasn't at all distracting.

She took down two crystal tumblers from the glass-fronted cabinets next to the liquor. Might as well go fancy tonight. It was a special evening.

"Mind pouring for us?" Inspired, she headed for a drawer where her mother had kept candles and selected a few of the small, thick ones that fit into glass cups to

shield the flames from the wind. A few Dove dark choc-
olates in a floral ceramic dish, a blanket her parents had
kept in a drawer by the door for just such occasions and
she was ready.

Out the back door, they went down the brick steps to
the pool level, where chaises were laid out on the concrete
deck ringed by trees.

On the table between two chaises, Kendra set up the
candles and lit them. The glow was lovely, the air soft.
Above them hung a moon, a bit more than a crescent,
sharp white against the sky's darkness. Around it a few
stars were just beginning to be visible. A hot man who
wanted her was settling beside her into a chaise, his long
hard body stretching to fill it.

Yes. Kendra was ready now. *Really* ready.

She reached across to clink glasses, tossed back a good
healthy swig of Woodford Reserve, loving the sweet burn,
the rich smoky aftertaste. "Jameson."

"Mmm?" He was savoring his whiskey properly.

"Would you like a chocolate?"

"Sure." He reached for the bowl; she stopped him with
an outstretched hand. "Let me."

He looked at her over the candles, their light flickering across his handsome face. Something in her expression must have communicated itself to him because he
shifted in his seat, took in a slow breath, then nodded.
"Be my guest."

The air around them turned electric. Distant city sounds
and the faint rush of surf traveled from down in the valley.
But up where they sat, all was silent except for the occasional whisper of a breeze through the trees.

Kendra got up and slowly unwrapped a chocolate
square, peeling back the foil on each corner before exposing it completely. She put the small square halfway
into her mouth, lips closed around its middle.

Jameson watched, only his eyes moving over her face, until she took a step toward his chaise. He moved to give her room to sit facing him.

"Kendra." His voice was low, husky, sensual. "That looks *really* good."

She planted a hand on his firm chest and leaned forward, expecting him to bite.

He didn't. He closed his lips over the other half of the square and dragged his tongue across the chocolate, moistening it, melting it, so the rich taste spread between them.

She was finding it hard to breathe, hard to think about anything but the nearness of his warmth, the heat of his body and her need for both.

The kiss deepened; their tongues tasted the candy and each other until the chocolate was liquid, then gone, and they were left only with increasing passion.

Strong arms came around her. Jameson pulled her onto his lap, stroking a line from her shoulder down her side, lingering over her bottom, then back up and across her front, lingering again between her breasts until she was aching for the feel of his fingers on them.

His hands slipped under her top, stroked up her back and unhooked her bra, then traveled around with maddening leisure toward her breasts.

Impatiently, she sat up, yanked her shirt over her head, slid off the bra and tossed it behind her.

"Touch me, Jameson."

His answer was a groan of satisfaction as his palms brushed over her nipples, then closed over her breasts. She arched into his touch, head back, eyes closed, the cool air around them intensifying the warmth of his skin.

He made her feel so beautiful, so alive, so powerfully sexy. As a woman she'd felt strong, capable, skilled and valued…but nothing like this.

She liked this. Increasingly, she liked everything about being with Jameson.

Except that he was still wearing clothes.

Her fingers tugged at the hem of his T-shirt, gray with the Dive 'n' Surf shop logo and colorful surfboards. Nice shirt. Kendra wanted it off. She wanted to feel her breasts pressed against the hard wall of his bare chest.

The shirt flew back over her head. In the dim candle-light his torso was indeed a work of art, warm and male. She lifted to straddle him, feeling the length of his erection hot and hard through the thin material of his shorts and her panties. She leaned forward, rubbed her breasts over the muscled landscape of his chest, loving the stimulation, the intimacy, the sheer animal pleasure of skin on skin, of touching and being touched.

Breath escaped him as if releasing it was both pain and pleasure. His hands traveled to her hips, under the elastic waistband of her skirt, finding and stroking her buttocks, moving her over his erection.

"You feel incredibly good, Kendra."

"Mmm." She kissed his neck, inhaling his scent, immersed in her senses. "So do you."

"I've wanted this since before I knew what it was."

She giggled, raising herself up to look at him, gently tracing his lips with her finger. "That long?"

"Look at you." He let his head fall back on the chair, pushing rhythmically under her, making her sway. "You are so beautiful."

With him she felt that way, inside and out. So when he sat up, saving her from pitching backward with strong arms on her back, and twisted them over until she was lying beside him on the chaise, then underneath, she went willingly.

This was what she wanted for both of them.

Starting at her calf, Jameson drew one hand up the

length of her leg, stopping to caress her sex through her panties, transferring warmth and pressure that made her feel less in control. Rather hot and desperate, in fact.

He lifted her skirt and wriggled down to kiss the material between her legs, his mouth warm and firm.

"Oh." She closed her eyes, a slight breeze fanning her heated cheeks. "That is amazing."

"So are you." Gently he pulled down her panties, exposing her to the night air. "And you're beautiful here, too."

His finger explored, stroking, touching, barely any pressure. Heat lightning traveled up her body. She forced herself to lie still, wanting to pull his head down to her, wanting him inside her, needing release from the building pressure.

They had all night.

His first kiss was so light she didn't recognize his lips until his tongue traveled up the length of her sex, parting her labia, ending with the lightest touch on her clitoris. Kendra's body jerked in reaction. She forced her breathing to slow, unfisted her hands, made her muscles relax.

Torture. The very sweetest kind.

He took his time, tiny touches and strokes with his fingers and tongue, adding to her arousal incrementally until she thought she'd go out of her mind. No one had ever taken time with her like this, the intensity building until an orgasm was simply inevitable.

"Kendra."

"Yes." She barely recognized the shaky tone as her own voice.

"I would like to make love to you."

"Yes."

The word exploded out of her, making him chuckle. "You don't sound very sure."

God, he was sexy. Looking at her with one eyebrow

quirked in pretend surprise, as if he had no idea what he'd been doing to her.

Then his smile faded. He undid his fly and stepped out of his clothes without ceremony, taking a condom packet from the back pocket of his shorts, rolling it on and sitting next to her, stroking her breasts, her stomach, gazing down at her body and then into her eyes.

"I've thought about this a lot, about how I thought it would feel with you. This is so much better. Better than my wildest fantasy." He waggled his eyebrows. "Some of them were pretty wild."

"Ooh." She drew her hand down the center of his torso. "You'll have to tell me about those."

"This is better because it's real. Of course. But also because it's finally you and me, Kendra. The place we've been heading to for a long time, I think longer than either of us suspects. Out in this garden where we can see the moon and hear the ocean and smell the eucalyptus." He put one hand on her heart, the other on his own. "You and me."

Kendra stared up at him. She could say nothing. What did he mean? He almost sounded as if...

He moved over her. She opened her legs for him automatically, not sure what was happening, why after all this time of good solid clarity, her mind was a whirl of confusion or why she had a sudden urge to cry.

His penis nudged at her sex; she reached down and guided him in, felt him push, stretch her, push farther, in and out until he was filling her completely. Her body responded. Her brain still couldn't grasp the moment or interpret her reaction.

Instinctively, she stopped trying, shut down her thoughts and concentrated on the sensations. The weight and motion of his body on hers, the welcome intrusion of his erection, the occasional caress of the breeze. The sweep of his broad back, the smooth planes of his skin, the swell of his buttocks, contracting and releasing. The climb of desire as he changed his motion, his rhythm, the force of his thrust, as if he was intent on experiencing every angle, every inch of her, inside and out, and had all the time in the world.

Sooner? Later? She couldn't tell. Only that at some point her response gradually changed; her body was no longer content with simple arousal. Her hips moved faster. She tilted her pelvis, squeezed her internal muscles to hold him tighter.

Jameson groaned and dug his hands under her buttocks, thrusting harder. A light perspiration broke out on Kendra's body; she felt her face flushing. She wrapped her arms around him, one hand gripping his side, the other clasping the back of his head.

The orgasm came on slowly, as if from a distance, gathered speed and power, rushing at her. She locked her legs around his, arched her back and let it sweep through her, holding herself rigid through the plateau of ecstasy, aware of Jameson's body gathering itself, as well. As she burst into contractions he gave a low shout, pushed once more and held still.

As if imitating the rise and fall of their climaxes, wind rose, gusted, then quieted again. Something rustled in the garden.

Kendra lay clutching Jameson's head, not wanting to let the moment go, aware of rising emotions that threatened to burst through her control. The steel wall was in danger.

He strained to lift his head; she made her fingers relax so he could, kept her eyes shut, concentrating on the smooth masculine feel of his body over hers, the tiny occasional pulsing aftershocks between their legs, some hers, some his.

This wasn't what was supposed to happen. She should be able to laugh now, to tease him, to smile and feel affec-

tion and relief and pleasure. Instead there was again a mass
of confusion and conflict she couldn't begin to understand.

"Look at me," he whispered.

She opened her eyes obediently to his, their blue shade
muted to gray in the darkness and flickering candlelight.

And then everything was clear.

With his arms around her she felt protected, safe, cared
for. For once she was not in charge. For once someone else
was taking the lead, watching out for her, keeping her safe.

Kendra enjoyed the revelation for all of about ten seconds, then the pleasure was replaced by the piercing pain
of vulnerability, more severe than she'd felt since right
after her parents died.

She was falling for him.

"I can't," she whispered, then realized she'd spoken
out loud and shook her head, no, no, no. Fear was making her stupid.

"Kendra." His brows drew down in concern. "You can't
what?"

"I don't know." To her horror, her voice was thick with
tears. God, no, she couldn't cry. He'd want to know what
was wrong. She couldn't tell him. She couldn't even begin
to tell him.

But the wave of grief was too powerful, too raw to be
contained. Tears ran hot down the sides of her face. She
pressed her fists over her eyes, as if the torrent could somehow be stopped. He'd think she was a lunatic.

He rolled off her and sat up. She didn't blame him.

"It's okay. It's okay." Strong arms drew her against him;
gentle hands stroked her hair. "Go ahead."

His sweetness undid her. She cried until her tear tank
was empty, for hours, it seemed. Through it all he held
her close, caressing her, murmuring words of support and
endearment. Never in her wildest dreams could she have

imagined Jameson Cartwright capable of such deep tenderness.

It only made her fall harder.

She clung to him until her sobs quieted, then forced herself to let go, to sit up, then stand. On her own two feet. To stop being a wet blanket weighing him down.

"Jameson." She couldn't begin to imagine what he was thinking. "I'm so sorry I lost it like that."

"Why?" He got up, too, took her hands, then slid his up her arms to cup the back of her neck.

"Well, I mean." She gestured stupidly at the chaise. "We were just… I mean, it's not like we were… It was supposed to be just fun. And playful. Like we are."

"It didn't turn out that way." He started massaging the tight muscles under his fingers.

"No."

"So?" He gave her that lazy smile. "That means there's more between us than fun. Nothing wrong with that."

"But… No, there isn't." She blurted out the words, then didn't blame him for smirking at her. "Okay, maybe."

He bent and kissed her. "I've got two bits of news for you."

"What?"

"One, there is something powerful between us and has been for a whole lot of years. So it makes perfect sense that making love would jar some emotion loose. Because it did in me, too."

"Only you didn't bawl all over me for an hour."

"I didn't lose my parents and have to take care of myself all alone for the past two years."

She scowled at him, but not with any real anger. Just because he was undoubtedly right. "What's the second thing?"

Jameson took her shoulders, looking deeply into her eyes. Her heart started a slow and steady thump. What was he going to say? Something deep. Something romantic and so wonderful she wouldn't be able to handle it.

He jerked his head over her left shoulder. "When you threw them, your bra and panties landed in the pool."

12

"I REALLY ENJOYED the show tonight."

"Thanks, Kendra." Matty grinned at her across their late-night table at Green Street Restaurant, liking her more and more. Granted, she'd only met her for the first time about fifteen minutes earlier, when she and Jameson had come to the stage door after the show, but she was one of those people who instantly appealed.

Not to mention Matty had never seen her brother so relaxed and outgoing and smitten. Around other girlfriends he'd always seemed vaguely apprehensive, as if awaiting judgment day. With Kendra he just looked happy. Matty might have had her last sleepless night over her baby brother for a while, though he and Kendra had a complicated future to work out, with Jameson about to go back to Keesler.

"How's the knee, Jamie?"

"Jamie?" Kendra gave Jameson an incredulous look. "I've never heard you called that."

"Ha!" Matty gestured to her brother with her wine. "There's worse. When he was little, we called him Jam-Jam."

Kendra clapped her hand to her mouth to muffle a snort, then lowered it and blinked sweetly at Jameson. "Jam-Jam... What a *lovely* name."

"Hilarious." Jameson rolled his eyes good-naturedly. "What about you, Fatty Matty?"

"Argh!" Matty clutched her chest. "Not that one!"

"Oh, ouch." Kendra winced in sympathy. "That is horrible. Especially since you're anything but heavy."

"Used to be."

"Ouch again." Kendra lifted her glass. "I'm a member of that club, too."

"Then you know. I think that nickname was one of Hayden's." Matty made her disgust plain. She and her twin brothers got along pleasantly now, but that was about it for closeness. They belonged to another era. "Kendra, what kind of insulting nicknames did you get hit with?"

"There's not much you can do with Kendra. My brother called me Kenny, not that clever, but it annoyed me so he did it. Mom and Dad just used endearments like honey or sweetie or ladybug. At school I got teased for being me." She patted Jameson's arm under the table. "Mostly by your brother."

Matty waved away the comment. "Boys are too dumb to show attraction in normal ways."

"We learn, though." The look he gave Kendra was pure adoration.

Kendra threw him a quick nervous smile and ducked her head.

Uh-oh. What was that? Embarrassed to show her feelings in front of the sister, or she wasn't quite feeling the big love yet?

If it was the latter, silly, silly girl. You didn't take that kind of devotion for granted, because it didn't strike often. No man had looked at Matty the way Jameson had just looked at Kendra for a long, long time. No one since Chris.

"Excuse me, guys, I'll be right back. It's been a long time since intermission." Kendra stood and headed for the restroom.

Matty beamed at her brother. "She's great, Jameson."

"Yeah, she's okay." His smile belied his casual tone. "I hear I have you to thank for siccing her on me."

"Me?" Matty thumped her hand to her chest. "I have no idea what you're—"

"I beat it out of her." He lifted his glass in a toast. "Thanks, Matty. You're a pain in the ass, but your heart is in the right place."

"Thank you, brother dear." She rested her chin on her hand and speared him with a look. "Have you gone over to see Mom and Dad yet?"

"I will." He shifted irritably. "I should, I know. And I will."

"How's Mike doing?" Matty had never met Mike, but would worship him forever because his apartment had saved Jameson from being driven crazy by their mom and dad during his recovery.

"He's loving the training. Working hard, studying hard."

"You'll get there." She watched his face carefully. He wasn't as hard to read as her other brothers, but still a tough one.

"It'll be a long haul. But yeah. They'll probably put me on a desk job until I'm ready to start up again."

"How will you and Kendra leave things?"

"Well, Ms. Nosy." He reached to tweak her nose, knowing she hated it.

"Off me, you pig." She reared back in plenty of time. "Now go on. You and Kendra…"

"Too soon to tell." He was all brisk business again, leaning back, stretching his legs to one side of the table.

"But you'd like to stay together."

"Yeah." He met her eyes, and Matty saw the vulnerability. Oh, gosh. He'd been through so much.

"She feel the same?"

"As I said, it's too soon to tell."

Matty nodded, heart aching. How could Kendra not fall for him? If she broke his heart, Matty would have to take her out personally. "Any chance you'll give up this Cartwright idea of devoting your life to the Air Force?"

"For that, I'll have to say it's too soon to tell." He checked over his shoulder to see if Kendra was on her way back yet.

"Right, right. Shutting up. Butting out." Matty flung herself back in her chair and buried her nose in her wine, gratified when he chuckled.

"You want to have lunch tomorrow? What is that, Saturday?"

"Mmm, I can't, I'm busy." Immediately she started blushing.

"Yeah?" He was watching her closely, which made her blush harder. "Who's this guy?"

"What guy?"

"Matty…"

Matty inhaled slowly. When she'd told Jameson about Chris shortly after they broke up, Jameson had come close to driving to Pomona to beat the crap out of him, more figuratively than literally. She hoped. But she couldn't lie to her younger brother. "Chris Hamilton."

"What?" His face crumpled into disbelief. "The Creepy Professor?"

"It's just lunch."

"What does he want?" Jameson was sitting straight now, all military posture and protective instinct. "How did he find you?"

She shrugged, *why does it matter?* "He came to my show. We talked after."

"Don't trust him."

She raised her left eyebrow. "Do I look stupid to you?"

"No. Sorry." He laughed shortly. "He just totally messed with you."

"Believe me, I remember." She put a finger to her chin as if she'd just thought of something profound. "Gee, kind of like you messed with Kendra in school."

"Oh, come on." He folded his muscled arms across his chest. She remembered when they'd been skinny sticks. "Not remotely comparable."

"No?"

"I was a kid doing stupid kid stuff out of unhappiness I didn't understand. He was a grown man—"

"Doing stupid grown-man stuff. I know. But he still swears nothing happened with Clarisse. And I know for a fact she was psycho."

"Oh, God." A look of horror grew on his face. "He's playing you. He still wants you."

"Am I interrupting?" Kendra approached the table and sat down, looking between them. "Uh. Should I go back to the bathroom?"

"No, no, you're fine." Matty giggled and held up her hand. "Jameson is in caveman mode because a guy who was horrible to me six years ago wants to have lunch."

"Really?" She looked at him curiously. "That horrible? Worse than you were?"

"Much." He glared at Matty, who grinned smugly. "You're going to give him another chance, aren't you?"

"Only if he earns it."

"I gave you one." Kendra nudged him with her shoulder.

"See?" Matty smiled appreciatively.

"It's not the same thing. This guy was her professor. He knew better."

"Excuse me." Matty raised her hand like a kid in class. "I knew better, too."

"He cheated on you with another student."

"Actually, that was just my assumption." Matty spoke calmly to balance her brother's temper. She'd laid it on thick six years earlier out of the horrible pain she was in, painting herself as the innocent victim and Chris as the heartless predator. She could see why Jameson wouldn't buy a new version now.

"She was naked in his apartment!"

"She was a very disturbed girl. He still says he didn't touch her."

Jameson's eyes narrowed. "How many times have you seen him?"

"Twice. We had drinks once, dinner the other night."

Kendra's head was going back and forth following the conversation.

"I can't believe this." He turned to Kendra. "What do you think?"

"Me?" Her eyes shot wide. "I'm not touching this one."

"No, I'm serious. You counsel people. You heard the problem. What do you think?"

Matty watched her, curious, nodding when Kendra turned her gaze to assess Matty's reaction.

"Bearing in mind I know almost nothing." Kendra laid her hand on Jameson's arm. "I'd say give your sister the benefit of the doubt here. I don't know this guy, and it sounds like what he did was a lot more serious than what you did, but I had certainly written you off, Jameson. Now that we're older, I can understand more of what you were going through and how you felt. But you think my father would be happy to find out I'm dating you now, after all the stuff I told him about you, all the times I came home in tears over something you'd done?"

"Woman logic." Jameson rested his head despairingly in his hands.

"She's just having lunch with him." Kendra patted him consolingly, giving Matty a wink. "I don't think that's so awful."

"Thank you, Kendra."

Jameson's head shot up. He glared at Kendra teasingly. "Yeah, thanks."

"I was talking to Mom yesterday." Matty spoke to change the subject, grateful for Kendra's support. "She's already baking and freezing pies for Thanksgiving."

Jameson chuckled. "Trust Mom to have it all under control."

"What's your Thanksgiving tradition, Kendra?" Matty's stomach sank the second the words left her lips. To someone who'd lost her family so recently, it was not the offhandedly polite question Matty meant it to be. "Sorry, that was awful. I wasn't thinking."

"No, no, it's fine." Kendra's smile was strained but genuine. "Last year I spent it with a friend's family. I think I'll just hang out at home this year."

"Come to ours." Jameson stroked her hair back from her face. "Food's great. And maybe Dad will convince you to enlist."

"You can wash dishes while the men watch football." Matty rolled her eyes. She'd given up trying to fight the gender inequity ingrained in her family culture, but it still drove her nuts.

"Oh, *that's* tempting." Kendra snorted.

"I help. Sometimes." Jameson's hand was gently massaging Kendra's neck. "I did once, anyway. I think last year I rinsed a fork."

Matty cracked up. This Jameson was new. She liked him very much. Watching him respond to Kendra's distress, the way he looked at her…

She was just plain envious.

Steady. Matty was not going to let herself jump into a relationship with Chris because she was lonely or because she hadn't been touched tenderly by a boyfriend in a long, long time and she craved it like crazy. Before tomorrow's lunch she'd need to have her list of reasons to go slowly, eyes open, intellect on full alert for a good long time. Only then would she permit herself to soften toward him.

Well, ahem, she'd softened pretty much like butter in the oven last time she saw him. But that was because she hadn't been forewarned or forearmed. Because she'd had champagne, because the night had been clear and beautiful and romantic and Chris was...Chris. Tomorrow they'd have a picnic lunch at Blaisdell Preserve, a public park ten minutes north of the Pomona College campus, emphasis on *public*. Daylight. No alcohol because she had a show that night. Not a setup for getting carried away.

She'd be cool, confident, calm and controlled.

Cool, confident, calm and controlled.

The words rang in her head as she sat behind the wheel of her Kia on her way out to Claremont, home to the Pomona campus and the very sexy Professor Chris Hamilton. The day was cool and hazy here by the coast, but farther inland when she reached the desert, the air would clear and temperatures rise. Southern California had it all.

She couldn't say she was entirely cool, confident, calm and controlled, but she was enough so that she'd come across that way. Machiavelli would approve. Inside she was tense, timid and in turmoil. The memory of the pain Chris had caused her battled with the memory of his arms around her Wednesday night in the downtown parking lot. Every time she thought of his lips on hers, a bolt of adrenaline got her attention in a serious way. A sexual way.

Oof. Maybe Jameson was right and this was a mistake. Matty just couldn't imagine putting her feelings for Chris to rest unless she faced him again and worked through the mess they'd gotten themselves in. Her hope was that, at the very least, she'd reach a place where she'd be better able to give another man her whole heart. The dating she'd done over the past six years had been an exercise in confusion and comparison. Not fair either to the guys she was seeing or to herself.

The trick was to define seeing Chris today as a new, healthy exercise, and let go of the persistent hope that she could give her heart back to the man who still held a piece of it.

She turned up the Patsy Cline CD she had playing and sang along with a Gershwin tune, clearing her mind of any complication. The haze was gradually lifting as she sped west on I-10, sharpening the beauty of the distant snow-dusted mountains, a welcome natural contrast to the traffic and urban sprawl close by. As she'd predicted, the air was warming, too. The temperature sensor on her car read in the low seventies, compared to the sixties close to the coast.

By the time she reached Claremont and had turned onto Harvard Avenue, she had managed to pull herself together internally, as well. She had all the power here. This was Chris's battle to fight. If he wanted her back, he'd have to work hard, regain her trust, prove himself worthy. She could sit back like the emperor at the Colosseum, thumb ready. Up? Okay, she'd give him another chance. Down? Hurl him to the lions!

On Seventh Street she slowed, looking for the right house number, heart pounding again. Normal to be nervous. It meant nothing. Getting close, closer…there. A charming house set back from the street, Craftsman style, painted deep green, with large trees and a nicely landscaped front yard.

Taking a deep breath, Matty swung the car to the curb and parked. Switched off the engine. Closed her eyes and counted to ten.

Then she opened the door and launched herself out, big smile on her face, clutching the container of cookies she'd offered to bring for their dessert—peanut butter–oatmeal–chocolate chip, made that morning while she sipped her coffee.

She approached the front door, raised her finger to stab the doorbell.

Cool, confident, calm and controlled.

The door opened, revealing Chris in thigh-hugging jeans and a loose maroon T-shirt, one hand on the door. His hair was damp from a recent shower, his eyes were clear and warm and he smelled like soap and shaving cream and man.

Crap. *Crap.*

"Hi." The syllable barely sounded. She had completely fallen apart, victim to a wave of lust so intense the only thing keeping her from flinging herself at him was that she'd drop the cookies.

He stepped back from the door; she crossed the threshold, fly into the spider's web, closing her eyes as she passed him, trying desperately to reconnect with the part of her that had been so strong seconds before. Where had it gone? How could she get it back?

Come on, Matty. She needed to break this tension, jump-start a normal, casual tone, start chatting, comment on the house, how it was in such good shape and how he'd done such nice things with it.

His hand took her arm. He turned her toward him, took the cookies from her stiff hands and laid the glass container gently on a table in his front hall.

She opened her mouth to say something, anything, but he pulled her toward him and kissed her, over and over, walking her back until she hit the wall and his body could press into hers.

Oh, that body. A man's body, fully formed, broadened, muscled and loaded with life and experience.

She kicked off her flip-flops one at a time, *thunk, thunk,* and gave in, wrapping her arms around his neck, realizing deep down she'd known this was going to happen, that this was why she was here, what she wanted more than anything.

Her hands found their way up under his shirt, to his chest, firm and sexy, a man's in the prime of life. He was eleven years older than she, but she had never felt so at home or natural with anyone else.

He had her cream-colored top off in seconds; his face rubbed the swells of her breasts while he unhooked her bra.

It slid off, leaving her breasts cool and sensual, exposed to his sight and his touch.

"Oh, Matty." He gazed reverently, cupping their weight, then took a lingering taste of her nipple, a hot sensation that shot down between her legs.

She whimpered, let her head drop back to rest against the wall, scrabbling her fingers over his shirt, bunching the material to take it off more easily.

The shirt pulled over his head; he straightened, a naked-torsoed god among men, and gathered her in his arms. She laid her head on his shoulder and stood still, listening to his breathing, as rough as hers, absorbing the familiar feeling of his skin on her skin, of her soft breasts pressed against his hard chest.

His sigh was a mixture of ecstasy and relief. Matty understood. She'd had one word running a loop through her brain: finally.

Finally.

"Do you want this, Matty? You're sure?"

"Yes." Her voice came out a husky groan. *"Yes."*

He released her, hands traveling down her sides as he slid to his knees, pressing his face against the flirty cotton knit skirt she'd pulled on that morning, wanting to look casual and sexy for him, but not as if she was trying to do either.

She fisted her hands, breath ratcheting up a notch, waiting for the heat of his mouth on her, the way he could make her come faster than a speeding bullet, with orgasms more powerful than a locomotive.

Oh, Chris.

His hands explored her waistband, then yanked the skirt down, her panties after; he buried his face between her legs, searching for and finding all the spots that would send her over the edge.

She lowered herself, spreading her legs, fisted his hair, urging him on, not that he needed encouragement. His tongue was driving her wild, bringing her close already.

"Yes." Her breath stuttered; her thigh muscles trembled. She pushed back against the wall, closing her eyes, bracing herself, waiting. She was close. So close.

The tongue stopped. Her eyes shot open to find Chris standing, hair disheveled, eyes hot with desire. He stepped forward and lifted her. She wrapped her legs around his waist as he carried her into his bedroom, laid her on the bed and proceeded to take off his jeans faster than it had ever been done by any human since the dawn of time.

With a small sense of satisfaction, she watched him retrieve a condom from a box on a high shelf in the back of his closet. Satisfaction because she got to watch the fabulous bunch and release of muscles in his back and very nice ass, but also because he wasn't keeping a big box right by the bed, available at a moment's notice.

Matty pushed the thought away as soon as she had it. This was about him and her and right now.

Condom on, he nearly dove back over her on the bed, making her giggle. "Been a while?"

"Six years."

She blinked in astonishment, then snorted. "Come on."

"Since I've been with *you,* Matty." He lowered his head and kissed her sweetly, tenderly, then again. "I've never stopped wanting to be with you."

No, no, no, none of that romantic stuff. They were here to screw each other because they couldn't keep themselves from doing it. That was all. That was enough.

She pulled his head down harder to deepen the kiss, spread her legs and tried to pull him over on top of her.

"Wait. I want to look at you." He put his hand at her collarbone and drew it slowly down her stomach to the hair between her legs, down one thigh, then the other, low as he could reach, following its progress with his eyes. "I've missed you."

"Um. I'm actually up here." She pointed to her head, wrinkling her nose at him, even knowing exactly what he meant, because she'd missed his body, too. And him.

He grinned and moved on top of her. "Trust me. I know where every inch of you is. How it likes being touched. And tasted. And loved."

Not that word.

He slid inside her, watching her face, filling her completely. She closed her eyes, taking deep breaths to keep from crying. She still loved him. She might always love him.

Then he started moving, and she concentrated with all her might on the sensations in her body so she could ignore those in her heart, pushing against his thrusts, savoring his size and shape, not too big, but enough that she knew he was inside her, felt him deep and hard, out and in, long thrusts alternating with smaller, gentle ones, bringing her closer every time.

Slowly, her thoughts were wiped clean; her body's hunger took over. She writhed underneath him, lifted her head, let it drop, sweat breaking on her skin, clutching at his back, panting and gasping for her climax.

And when it came, it bore down on her with astonishing power, a shaft of hot sweetness that built nearly unbearably, making her strangle a scream in her throat. Then the beautiful release, vaginal muscles contracting around his penis. He paused to feel her coming, then pushed again savagely until his body arched and his mouth opened in a silent yell. She didn't have to look. She knew how he came. She knew so much about him.

Except whether he'd break her heart again.

13

KENDRA LAY IN her bedroom, Jameson spooned behind her, his arm draped protectively over her waist. She hadn't slept well, and when she finally drifted off she'd had another nightmare. This time she wasn't watching Jameson be shot by a sniper or exploded by an IED. This one took place on Thanksgiving at the Cartwrights', only the house had become a huge, columned, Southern-style mansion. She'd had to pass between his parents on one side and his leering brothers on the other, one of whom took pictures while the other took her measurements with a tape and called out the numbers with immense disappointment.

At dinner, a sneering servant placed a thirty-pound turkey in front of Kendra, who was expected to carve with an antique sword. Jameson hadn't been there, but as she'd tried to hack pieces off the bird, which slipped and skated around the platter, the Cartwrights' phones had rung in unison with the announcement of Jameson's death—crushed under a load of mashed potatoes tipped from a truck. Driven by a cat.

Amusing, except in the dream the emotions had been very real. Foreigner in a family that didn't belong to her. Panic in a situation she could normally handle—she'd helped her dad carve the turkey once she was old enough for knives. And the wrenching pain of that phone call.

She blinked away tears and screwed her eyes shut, angry at her subconscious for doing this to her.

"Kendra?" The worried whisper was barely loud enough to hear. "You okay? You were making funny noises."

"I'm fine." She tried to speak normally. "Bad dream."

"Yeah?" He stroked her, embrace tightening, hand traveling up between her breasts. It was an effort not to flinch. His arm felt like a vise. "What about?"

"I can't remember." She needed to get up, move around. She'd be fine. It was just another dream. Kendra hadn't yet accepted Jameson's Thanksgiving invitation. She didn't have to meet his family. She didn't have to get into this relationship any deeper than she was already. Jameson would leave in a week and a half. She'd get over him and move on, be fine on her own again, helping people, enjoying her friends. A good, productive life. And when she was ready to get serious about someone, she would. Not now. Not yet. "Be right back."

She wiggled out of his embrace, jumpy and irritable, used the bathroom, then grabbed her short nightie from the hook behind the door and crossed the foyer and dining room into the kitchen to slip out onto the deck.

It was chilly, low sixties probably, maybe high fifties. She hugged her arms around her chest, trying to calm herself, gazing out past the city's twinkling lights toward the blackness of the ocean, imagining its vast, peaceful depths.

The door opened behind her. A flash of annoyance made her close her eyes. It wasn't Jameson's fault. None of this was his fault.

"Hey." He stepped out onto the deck with her, gloriously naked. Lucky neighbors.

"Hi." She gestured out toward the view. "I was just wanting some air."

"What's bugging you, Kendra?"

"Me? Nothing." She shook her head. "The dream was upsetting. I guess I was just feeling—"

"If you don't want to tell me, that's fine. But quit the B.S."

She took in a sharp breath, drawing herself up, opened her mouth for a rude retort, then deflated abruptly. "Yes. Okay. Sorry."

His hands were on his lean hips. She could see in the dim glow traveling up from the night-lights around the pool that his features were drawn with worry. He was so handsome, her naked airman, eyes narrowed, strong chin slightly jutted, full lips compressed. "It's cold out here. You need something warmer?"

"I can't go to your parents' house for Thanksgiving, Jameson."

A gust of wind sent leaves scuttling across the deck. "Okay."

"I don't want to get serious with you."

He jerked back slightly—or did she imagine it? She'd blurted the words out, not even aware they were on their way to her voice box. But maybe if she had to hurt him, it was better to do it sooner rather than later.

Jameson nodded slowly. "Understood about Thanksgiving. And not getting serious, yeah, I get that, too. Easier, actually, since I'll be leaving."

"Yes. Yes, exactly." She should feel relieved. She didn't. If anything she felt more keyed up, angrier, more panicky. "Since you're leaving."

"That it?"

"I think so." She nodded, relaxing a bit, realizing she'd subconsciously expected some kind of battle. Or a strong reaction, anyway. So he hadn't wanted to get serious either. Well, good. That was good. "I mean, yes. That's it."

"So." He folded his arms across his magnificent chest.

"Are you really intent on freezing to death, or can we get back into bed?"

"Jamie…"

He looked surprised, either because of the nickname or the fact that it came out sounding as though she was about to do something desperate.

She wasn't. But she wanted to. Pressure was building in her chest, in her throat. She wanted to do something totally desperate, scream or throw something.

"What is it?" He took a step toward her. Her panic increased, her breathing quickened.

And then, looking up at him, at his amazing nakedness, she knew exactly what she wanted to do.

"I want you to make love to me."

He gave a short laugh. "Kendra, that is never, ever a problem."

"Out here." She turned to the railing, grabbed the wooden bars, flipped up her nightie and bent forward. "Like this."

She heard him mutter under his breath. Then his hands were on her hips; he pressed his pelvis up against the crevice between her legs. "Like this?"

"Yes." All her anger, all her frustration and all her passion were suddenly channeled into intense arousal, intense need for this man and his cock inside her. She separated her feet more, bent down farther. "Now."

He groaned faintly. "I don't have a condom."

"I don't care."

"Yes, you do. I do, too. Hang on."

Hang on. Literally. She pressed her forehead against the wood, breathing hard, body chilling, face hot, feeling the soft breeze tickling her sex. She wanted him this way, behind her like an animal, hard and barbaric, with no chance for her to fall for him any farther than she already had.

His footsteps sounded on the deck behind her. She closed her eyes, waited.

Hands on her hips, fingers spreading her labia, then the strong push inside her, slightly painful, stretching her hard, but good pain, exciting pain, exactly what she wanted. "Yes. Yes, take me. Hard."

He did as she asked, moved forcefully, thrusting, hands pinioning her hips, making her arms work to keep her steady. She closed her eyes, reveling in his power, his masculinity and his control—giving her the ride of her life without real danger.

She wanted danger. "C'mon, Lieutenant. Give it to me."

He grunted harshly, renewed his grip. She reached back, cupped his balls in her hand and squeezed. He was working her hard, erection banging her cervix with the longest thrusts, making her gasp with the sharp pain, then relax into it, increasing her pleasure and the sense of risk.

Along with her arousal, the wildness grew. "Don't come. I don't want you coming. I want you hot and hard and giving it to me the rest of the night."

He gave a hoarse shout, stopped pushing, held still, panting, holding off his climax.

"What's the matter, Jameson?" She pushed back onto him, controlling the movement herself.

"Wait, Kendra."

"I'm not waiting," she whispered savagely. "I'm going to keep you pumping me."

"Wait." He grabbed her firmly, kept her still in spite of her struggle to move, in spite of her hands caressing his balls, in spite of her furious whispering.

Then he gave a low groan and drove into her again and again, breath coming wet and harsh through his clenched teeth.

"Can you feel me, Jamie? How tight I am? Can you feel my muscles squeezing your cock?"

"Yes." He spit the word out, his legs tight as metal rods behind her.

"Don't come. Don't come. Don't come." She reached farther, found the spot under his ball sac, the very base of his penis, the magic spot that would increase his arousal to a point even he couldn't resist.

"Damn it, Kendra. You're going to make me lose—" He stiffened, gave a moan of surrender that turned into a low desperate shout as he plunged viciously inside her, once, twice, again, and came, pulsing, panting, fingers digging into her hips, giving her a fierce sense of power and satisfaction. Yes. *Yes.*

She had control here; she was not the vulnerable one, she was strong and in charge of herself and of her feelings.

Jameson laid his hand on her lower back, his breath slowly returning to normal. A cold, damp breeze swept them, making Kendra shiver. Her back was stiffening. Her sex was raw and throbbing, still aroused.

Oh, God. She was completely losing it.

"Jameson." Her whisper sounded desperate again. Who was in control? Of what?

He pulled out of her gently, helped her straighten, then without missing a beat, bent and threw her over his shoulder. Ignoring her shocked squeal, he strode back through the warm house into her bedroom, where he laid her on the bed and opened her legs, shoved his face between them.

She gasped with the surprise of it, the sudden pleasure, gripping his head as he painted her all over with his tongue, putting in extra time, heat and pressure on her clitoris, fingers pushing gently inside her, searching, exploring.

"Don't come, Kendra. Don't you dare." His fingertips began massaging a spot deep in the front of her vaginal wall.

She made an inarticulate sound, tried to back down,

back away, back off, but his lips, his fingers—she wasn't going to be able to. He shifted the spot; her desire climbed exponentially. She gave up, gave in, gave a short scream, lifting her hips off the bed, the orgasm making her convulse around his fingers and under his tongue, the pleasure lengthening, even as it decreased in intensity. Again and again until she couldn't come anymore.

"Okay." She panted out the word, then started to laugh, slightly maniacally. "Okay. We're even."

"Yeah?" He kissed his way up to her mouth, covering her with his body, covering them with sheets and blankets. "I wasn't keeping score."

"I was. I always do." She put a hand to the side of his face to show she was teasing. Soft, smooth skin, scratchy stubble. A face becoming dear to her. One she'd miss. Dear Lord, what was she doing to herself?

"Good to know."

Kendra laughed again, still sounding crazed, put her hands up to push back her hair, then kept them clamped to the sides of her head. She was going nuts. From sad to restless to depraved, to miserable, to sexual and now... she wasn't even sure what she felt now, other than sexually sated. "I think I have multiple personality disorder. Or, I don't know, what other mental illness has wild mood swings?"

"There's one you should know about."

"Uh-oh." She blew out a breath, lowered her hands. "What is it?"

"Grief."

Kendra let her hands drop, nearly bonking Jameson with her elbow. "Maybe you're right."

"Of course I'm right!"

She giggled, turning toward him, lying close enough that their noses were nearly touching. "I guess I'm not done with that."

"With all you had to cope with, I bet you put some of it off. Maybe a lot of it."

"Stop doing my job." She smiled at him, reached to touch those lovely, sensual lips, fighting another wave of panic at the thought of him going so far away from her so soon.

Not tonight. Tomorrow was another day, as her mom would say. Tonight she had a sexy naked airman in her bed. That would be enough for now.

"Jameson."

"Mmm?"

"Tell me what you're most afraid of."

Jameson groaned. "This again?"

"This again."

He kissed her, started stroking her hair away from her face, hypnotic, rhythmic stroking that made her want to melt into the mattress. "Let's see…"

Kendra's heart flipped. Would he joke again or really answer this time?

"I'm afraid after I leave that you'll have moments of sadness or fear or uncertainty and I won't be here to help you through them."

She caught her breath. Oh, gosh. His worst fear was purely on her behalf. Now she *really* was going to melt into the mattress. "But I'm invincible. Nothing can hurt me."

"And I'm afraid I'll go back to the Air Force and realize it's not my whole life's ambition anymore."

"That's a hard one." She put her hand to his chest. "But you're not locked in for twenty years, right? I mean, you could get out sooner if you wanted."

"It's a four-year minimum commitment. So yes, I could leave earlier."

"Have you considered it?" She tried not to sound hopeful. His life, his decision, and it would still mean he was leaving.

"Yes."

Her chest squeezed tight. "Because of your injury?"

"Because of what you brought to my life, Kendra. And because of you." His stroking moved down her suddenly stiffened back, his fingers warm and sensual on her skin. "Shh, don't panic. Breathe. You have at least four years without me around. I'm handing you your not-serious on a silver platter."

"Huh." She kissed him, sweetly, letting him know with her lips what his words had meant to her. He was just talking, he'd made no decisions. She'd take this as a lovely compliment.

Jameson deepened the kiss, rolled over on top of her. "Want to come with me?"

"To Keesler?"

"You bet!" He nodded, puppy-dog eagerly. "And then wherever they send me for the next four lo-o-ng years?"

She snorted. "*How* is that not getting serious?"

"Oh, right. I forgot. How about instead we get engaged? Tomorrow work for you?"

"Jameson." She cracked up.

"What. You want to get married right away?" He deliberately let more of his weight pin her to the mattress, digging his arms tightly around her. "Geez, give a guy some space, would you?"

"Stop!" She pushed at his dead weight. "Bad Jam-Jam!"

"Don't ever, *ever* call me that." He lifted off slightly, his threat made idle by the laughter brimming in his voice. "Or else."

"Or else what?"

"I'll make love to you until you beg for mercy."

"Oh!" She frowned, pretending to reconsider. "Wait, is that supposed to be punishment?"

"Not tonight. It's late." He rolled off and turned her on her side, curled behind her as he'd been when she first woke from her nightmare, only this time his arms didn't feel threatening or confining, but comforting and secure. "I want you to get some sleep."

Kendra smirked in the darkness. "I hear and obey, oh great and powerful Jam-J—"

"Kendra."

She giggled and adjusted her body against his, checking in with all the places they were pressed together. Calf to shin. Bottom to groin. Back to chest. Skin to skin. "Good night, Jameson."

"Good night, my beautiful."

She took a deep breath and blew out the last of her tension and fear, aware of a growing sweetness in her chest. A contentment like she'd never felt before. And if she wasn't so tired and drained, and if she hadn't had such an emotional workout tonight, she'd probably be panicking all over again.

Because it was a lot harder to keep yourself from being serious about a guy when you were already falling in love with him.

14

KENDRA JOGGED NEXT to Lena down the strip of pavement marking the beginning of the South Bay bike trail in Torrance, the neighboring town to Palos Verdes Estates. On her left the ocean hurled itself relentlessly toward them. On her right, tourists and residents strolled or drove down the esplanade, lined with palm trees, apartments and condos.

"Whoa, honey." Lena touched her arm and slowed, her shorter legs scrambling to keep up. "Are we training to win a marathon here?"

"Sorry." Kendra pulled back. She was pushing her usual pace, hoping to exhaust herself to the point where she could sleep better at night.

"What's going on? You seem tense. Things been going okay with soldier boy?"

"Airman." She corrected her without thinking. "Yeah, they're okay."

"Hmm. I'm not exactly blown away by your enthusiasm."

Kendra stopped herself from speeding up again. "I don't want to get serious with him."

"Given that he's leaving in six days, that sounds reasonable."

"It is. It is totally reasonable."

Lena gave her a sidelong look. "He giving you trouble over it?"

"No." She was startled by the underlying bitterness in her response, and brightened her tone. "No, not at all."

"His sister giving you trouble?"

"Matty? No. She seems fine."

"So?" Lena beckoned more words out of her. "What's the problem?"

"I don't know." Kendra made a sound of exasperation. "I don't know what's wrong with me. I'm a complete mess, mood swings all over the place, impatient one second, crying the next."

"You pregnant?"

"God, no. No, no. I'm on the pill and we use condoms." She snorted. "I think it must be something simpler. Like a brain tumor."

"Oh, there's a nice thought." Lena wiped her perspiring face on the shoulder of her bright red shirt, which fell halfway down her thighs and probably belonged to Paul. "Maybe you're going through something else hormonal. Menopause?"

"At twenty-four?"

"Hmm, guess not." She touched Kendra's elbow. "You missing your parents?"

"Yeah." Her voice choked up. "I bet this fling with Jameson has stirred that up, too."

"Hmm."

They jogged in silence for a while, passing two women with strollers.

"One thing bothers me, Kendra."

"What's that?"

"This thing about not wanting to get serious." She blew at a strand of hair that had escaped her sweatband. "Why would you say that?"

"Because I don't want to get serious? He leaves, he leaves for years. This isn't some brief absence."

"Yeah, but…" They parted company around a pair of

walkers. "If it's right, you could work something out. Tons of military couples do. It sounds like you're being defensive."

"Against what?"

"Oh, I don't know. Maybe the fact that you're falling for him."

"I *am* falling for him." The sentence came out close to hysterical; she forced her voice calmer. "That's the whole problem."

Lena burst out laughing. "Here I was braced for rabid denial. That's great, Kendra. Seems like he's really good to you. And he's not exactly a hardship to look at."

"I don't want to get serious."

"You know, I've heard that about you."

Kendra giggled. "On the news?"

"Do you think he's serious about you?"

"He invited me to his family's Thanksgiving."

"Oh." Lena blew at the strand again. "That is serious. You going?"

"No."

"Why not?"

"Too serious."

Lena cracked up. "We are apparently antiserious! But also maybe…because it's a family holiday and he's got a family, complete with parents. You had a hard time even at my house last year."

"Maybe that, too. I don't know, Lena, that's what is making me nuts. I just don't know. Can we change the subject?"

"No."

"Lena…"

"Okay, okay. How about them Raiders? Think they'll get into the playoffs this year?"

Kendra rolled her eyes. Lena knew she didn't follow football. "I'm sure they will. Unless they don't."

"Here's something I need to tell you…" Lena's voice slowed, became guarded.

Kendra turned to look at her and nearly tripped over a kid chasing a ball onto the pavement. "What?"

"I might not be able to do these runs much longer."

Kendra's stomach dropped. "Why not? Is something wrong? You're not moving, are you? You're not…sick?"

"No!" Lena waved her arms as if to erase what she'd said. "No to both. It's a good thing. Maybe. Maybe someday soon."

Kendra took one look at her friend's face, radiant under her boyish haircut, and gasped. "You're pregnant?"

"Not yet." She patted her abdomen, grinning. "But we've decided to start trying."

"Wow!" Elation filled Kendra, which felt much better than the emotional cesspool she'd been floundering in before. "This is wonderful. Lena, I'm so excited for you. Both of you."

"Thanks. Who knows. It may take a while, but we're ready."

"Will you quit your job when the baby comes?"

"Uh." She held up her hand. "One thing at a time. We only just decided to try."

"Oh, Lena, it's really great. You and Paul will have a family." She jogged three more paces and burst into tears, then started laughing. "See? I've gone completely nuts."

"Honey? Can I say something you might not like?"

"Yes, of course." She sniffed and wiped the tears, struggling for control. "Anyone else I might take out, but you always can."

"I think you're past falling for him. I think you're in love with this guy. As in serious."

"No. No." Even as she protested, something inside her relented. "God, Lena, what am I going to do?"

"Why do you have to *do* anything? Just enjoy it."

"Because I don't want to be involved right now. I'm not ready. It's too soon. He's leaving and it will be horrible and sad and awful missing him. I don't want to miss anyone. I *hate* doing that."

Lena caught Kendra's hand and slowed them to a walk, her brown eyes anxious. "Shh, okay."

Kendra closed her eyes, blew out a breath. She loved him. Of course she did. She had for a long time, maybe even back in school, though she'd been entirely too proud and stubborn to admit it.

"You can't tell your heart what to feel." Lena led Kendra off the pavement, onto the sand, squeezed her hand and let go. "If this guy is right for you, he's right. And maybe he's most right if he's leaving, because then he won't be in your face all the time and you can continue to heal while you have his support."

"But he'll be in the Air Force. He could…trip over more cats." She waited for her friend's shout of laughter. "I couldn't stand to lose him."

"That's what love is, honey. Massive, unbearable vulnerability."

"Well, ick, why does anyone do it?"

Lena gave a blissful sigh. "Because, sweetheart, in all of life, there is simply nothing better."

"You're right. I just wish I could get rid of the fear." Kendra echoed Lena's sigh, but hers wasn't blissful. "I'm being really whiny and annoying, aren't I?"

"Tremendously." Lena led the way back to the path. "Remember when Paul broke up with me the year before we got married? Remember how I was then?"

"Ugh." Kendra made a face. "Unbearable."

"See? You owe me." By mutual consent they started running again. "Have you talked to Jameson about this?"

"All I've told him is that I don't want to get serious. Since then we have just been enjoying each other."

Lena shrugged. "Start with what you feel now, even if it's just laying out your confusion. Don't go farther than that. It's like this baby. We can think about his or her entire life now and drive ourselves into a complete panic… or we can just have a lot of really great sex and see what happens."

"I see your point. Especially about the sex."

"Yeah, you guys do okay, I can tell by seeing you together. Unlike that last guy you dated, what was his name?"

"Grant." Kendra blew a raspberry. "Old Faithful. Same time, same position, same…"

"Do *not* say eruption."

Kendra laughed, feeling more stable, more optimistic and eternally grateful to her friend. "I'll talk to Jameson. Thanks, Lena."

"You're welcome. It's scary giving your heart to someone, but if he's right for you, you'll do it no matter what." She swerved closer to nudge Kendra with her elbow. "So you might as well woman up and admit it."

JAMESON GAVE HIS nervous mother a kiss on her soft cheek and shook hands with his scowling father. The visit, his first since he'd been back in town, had gone well. At least for him. He hadn't squirmed and mumbled under his father's crossfire over his physical therapy routine and gradual return to normal daily activity. He'd answered clearly, honestly and for the first time, his dad's bluster and puffery hadn't bothered him. Dad had done basic training on an injured hamstring? Good for him. Jameson's older brother had recovered completely from shoulder surgery and was back flying within weeks? Hayden was amazing. Jameson was glad for him. Mark didn't think twenty years in the Air Force sounded like enough? Jameson wished him all the happiness in the world. But over the past few days he'd come to see clearly that four would be enough for him.

"Thanks for lunch, Mom. I'll see you Thursday. I'll bring wine." He wished he could say he'd be bringing Kendra.

"Bye, Dad, see you Thursday."

His father nodded curtly, shook his hand and slapped him on the shoulder, his equivalent of a hug. His dad would get over his disappointment eventually. More important, he'd figure out that his youngest son was his own man, sure of what he wanted. Jameson had Kendra to thank for a lot of that. Her crazy questions and her insistence that he get up off his poor-me ass and take a look around him had done more than break his depression. They'd given him the impetus to take a look at his life, too, and to choose what he really wanted to fill it with.

Mostly he wanted to fill it with Kendra.

Jameson nodded to his parents and turned to climb into the SUV he'd rented when he'd gotten sick of having to depend on other people for transportation.

He pulled out of his parents' driveway and headed south on Via Cataluna. An idea had come to him the previous evening, a way he could ease some of Kendra's conflict and get some resolution himself. It might be a colossally bad idea, but he didn't have any others. She seemed caught between what her mouth and words told him—that she did not want to get serious—and what her body and actions told him—that she was falling as far and as hard as he was.

Or so he hoped.

So what should he do? Back off, leave town and send her a how-are-ya email once in a while from Keesler and then whatever base they sent him to next?

There was only one person in the world he could talk to about this. He'd been meaning to call Matty today anyway, to find out how things were going with the Creepy Professor. He'd wanted to call every day, hell, he'd wanted to tag along on their dates with his service weapon…but she was an adult and, like all of them, had her own stupid mistakes to make.

Or not. He hoped not.

She picked up on the second ring. "Hey, Jameson, how was lunch?"

"It was fine. Dad was Dad. Mom was Mom."

"I'm so surprised!"

"I told them I'm not reenlisting after this contract expires."

She gasped. "Jameson, wow. I'm...okay, I'm thrilled. But only if you're sure it's what you want."

"I'm sure."

"How did Dad take it?"

"Pretty much the way you'd expect. But I let it roll over me."

"Good for you, Jamie. I know how hard it is to let Dad roll. But good for you. I'm really happy that you're standing up for—" She gasped again, louder this time. "Is this because of Kendra?"

He smirked. Looked like his segue had just been handed to him. "Are you kidding me? You think I'd change my life for a woman? What kind of wimp do you—"

"I knew it! This is awesome! Have you talked to her yet?"

"That's kind of why I'm calling."

A third gasp. "You asked her to marry you!"

"Who-o-oa, there, Nellie." He did his best cowboy imitation, which admittedly wasn't very good. "She is not in any place to ask right now. She freaked out when I invited her for Thanksgiving. You saw her."

"But if she were in a place to ask, would you?"

He pulled over, parked the car and reclined his seat. "I refuse to answer on the grounds that it's none of your business."

"Which is why you called me to talk about it."

"Oh. Yeah. That." He shoved his hand through his hair, thinking he'd have to make an appointment for a cut before he showed his face back at Keesler. "First tell me how things are going with Creepy."

"Chicken."

"You're having chicken?"

"No, *you're* chicken. I'm having…complications."

"Matty." He struggled upright, not comfortable relaxing when his sister might need him to drive to Claremont and punch someone. "What's going on?"

"We're having nice times, actually. Really nice. Whether or not he's right for me, whether or not I'm a masochistic idiot, there is still something really big going on between us."

He wanted to growl. "Okay."

"But even after all these really nice times…" She sighed.

"You still can't totally trust the bastard."

"Not completely. At the same time, Jameson…" She growled in frustration. "I really need to come up with a way to put this to rest, or I'm going to kill any hope of having something special with this man. Essentially, I'm killing any happiness we might have because of crap I can't stop worrying about that might not even be a problem."

"Or it might."

"Or it might. But guilty until proven innocent is not a good basis for any relationship."

"True." He frowned thoughtfully. Something important was circling in his head, looking for a place to settle.

"I confronted him when we first hooked up again, we've talked it over and he has a logical explanation. Either I have to reject that explanation and leave him, or accept it and leave him alone. This is my crap. I have to own it."

Jameson opened the car door. He couldn't sit still any longer. "Is there anything *he* could do that would help you deal with this?"

"Yes." She laughed dryly. "One thing. About as likely as a solar eclipse."

"What's that?" He knew her answer before she said it, knew that she'd been the right person to call, knew his next stop and what he'd say to Kendra next time he saw her.

"He could tell me he wants to marry me."

MATTY PULLED UP to the small Mediterranean-style house on Oak Avenue in Manhattan Beach and whistled softly. Two million, easy, in this town. Clarisse had done very well for herself. Or found a man who had.

She parked in front of the house and turned off the Kia's engine, wrinkling her nose. This was probably one of the more risky ideas she'd ever had. It could turn out a dozen different ways. She hadn't called to let Clarisse know she was coming. She didn't want to give her former friend any time to prepare for the encounter, or guess any of the reasons Matty was coming. And in case Matty decided this was one of the worst ideas she'd ever had, she wanted to be able to ditch it with no consequences.

Talking to Jameson the day before had gotten her thinking. Saying out loud that she wished she could come up with a way to put her doubts about Chris to rest had made the solution pop into her head. Only one person could corroborate Chris's version of what Matty had seen that day six years ago. The problem, of course, was that Clarisse might still be as unreliable as she'd always been. In which case Matty would be back to square one.

Nothing ventured, nothing gained, as Mom would say.

So it was venture time. She grabbed her purse and got out of the car, self-consciously smoothing the hem of her favorite teal top and fluffing her hair, wishing she'd gotten it trimmed. She laughed at her vanity. As if her outfit or hairstyle would make any difference. What a complication she and Jameson had made of their love lives. How

long since their biggest concern was whether Mark and
Hayden were cheating at Monopoly?

Someday they'd both be happily married and laugh at
these worries, too. She hoped.

Blowing out a breath, Matty forced herself to start toward the front door, telling herself Clarisse could easily
not be home, so she might not have to face this confron-
tation today after all. Her next thought was that Clarisse
had better be home, because she wanted this confronta-
tion the hell over with.

On the front step, she made herself jab the doorbell
without stopping to think, because otherwise she might
stand there agonizing forever.

Two seconds went by.

Clearly Clarisse wasn't home. Matty could just turn
around now and—

The door opened.

She was home.

Still beautiful, still slender, the kind of face that drew
men's glances, wide-set blue eyes and shoulder-length
nearly jet-black hair that spilled over itself in a silky cascade when she tipped her head.

Her lovely dark brows drew down. "May I help— Oh,
my gosh, *Matty!*"

"Hi, Clarisse." Matty was suddenly overcome with emotion. Before she'd started to clue in to the depth of Clarisse's issues, they'd had a lot of fun together early in their
senior year—midnight beer runs, working out together,
seeing movies, writing crazy poetry, trying out for shows
on campus, talking until four in the morning.

So when Clarisse burst into tears and went to hug her,
Matty did the same.

"I am completely undone. I can't believe you're here."
Clarisse sniffed and wiped her eyes with long pink-nailed
fingertips. "Come in. Please, come in."

Matty followed her into the living room: exposed beams in the ceiling, hardwood floors, a brick fireplace and an unusual collection of modern paintings. "What a gorgeous house."

"Thanks." Clarisse turned as if seeing the room for the first time. "The art is mostly John's. My husband. I met him— Gosh, Matty, we have so much to catch up on."

Matty nodded, guilty at Clarisse's warmth when she was primarily here to ask if she'd screwed Matty's boyfriend six years earlier. Of course, with Clarisse, you never quite knew what was real. This Clarisse did seem calmer, more self-possessed. And if she'd gotten married, maybe she was doing better. Or maybe her husband was nuttier than she was.

"Would you like a beer?" Clarisse grinned mischievously. "I have our favorite, Sierra Nevada Pale Ale."

"I'd love one." She gave a hyperenthusiastic double thumbs-up, their sign for a good time and place for beer, at the same time Clarisse did.

A few minutes later, Clarisse was back in the living room with a tray on which stood two opened beers—both of them preferred to drink straight from the bottle—a bowl of pretzels, a plate of baby carrots and a hunk of what looked like really good cheddar with some crackers.

"Sit, sit. Help yourself." She put the tray on the spotless glass-topped coffee table and sat on the white couch, her simple red top, diamond solitaire necklace and slim black pants making a stunning contrast. "Matty, I about fell down when I saw you at the door. I've thought about you so many times, thought of picking up the phone, but I figured you didn't ever want to see me again."

"Oh." Matty fingered the label of her beer, then took a swallow. "I'm actually here for a reason besides just catching up."

"Okay." Clarisse abruptly uncrossed her legs and reached for a pretzel.

"It's about Chris."

Clarisse met her eyes, then looked away. She put the pretzel on her napkin. "I thought it might be."

"I bumped into him a few weeks ago."

"Really." She was speaking cautiously, holding her body tight. "When did you last see him?"

"At Pomona. Senior year."

Her face fell; her hand crept to the diamond resting on her chest. "Matty, I…I hoped you'd get back together someday."

"We didn't." She watched Clarisse closely, saw her struggle to keep back tears. "I couldn't trust him after I found him with you."

"But I wrote to you explaining." She got up from the couch and stood by the mantel, three-quarters turned away. "Didn't I write to you?"

"No. Saying what?"

She faced Matty in obvious distress, hand still at her throat. "So many things are still…missing or confusing from that time. I thought I wrote you a letter a month or so after graduation. Or maybe an email. In it I told you about that night and begged you to forgive me."

Forgive what? "If you did, I never got it."

"I don't know, maybe I dreamed it or hallucinated." She laughed bitterly. "Well, that explains why you never answered. I thought you'd written me off."

"I did." She smiled to take the sting out of the words.

"I meant after you found out what really happened."

Matty made herself count to three. "What really happened?"

"You probably figured out I'm bipolar."

Matty winced. No, that wasn't the truth she was after,

but Clarisse was due genuine sympathy. "I'm sorry. I knew you were struggling."

"That's a nice way to put it." She strode back to the couch and sat again. "I'm on meds now. I'm doing really well. But back then I did a lot of really messed-up things that still haunt me. Trying to seduce Chris was a big one."

Matty took a casual sip of beer. "Trying?"

"I was jealous of you." Clarisse lifted her hand, let it flop down on the couch cushion. "I wanted what you had."

Did you get it? She nodded, unsure how else to respond.

"I know it makes no sense, not even to me anymore. But back then in my twisted way of looking at life, it was pure logic."

"I'm sorry to make you talk about all this again." Matty smiled grimly, getting impatient. "But I need to ask—"

"No, no, talking about it is really fine. I feel so much better knowing you never got my letter." She made a face and shuddered dramatically. "If I even *sent* one."

"I'm sure you—"

"Which it looks now like I didn't." Clarisse sighed, shaking her head, hair sliding out of place, then settling back to perfect. "Honestly, Matty, having a mental illness stinks."

"I'm really sorry, Clarisse." She bit her lip. "And I'm so glad you're in a better place now. But I—"

"I'm a new person." She grinned and stretched her slender arms up over her head. "I have my husband, John, to thank for that. He's a remarkable—"

"Clarisse." Matty held up her hand to stop the chatter. "I need to know if he slept with you."

Clarisse gaped in astonishment. "Who, John?"

"No, Chris!"

"Chris?"

"Yes! Chris!"

"No, of *course* not. He didn't even touch me." She looked at Matty as if *she* was the one with a mental illness. "He was crazy in love with you."

15

KENDRA CHECKED THE half turkey breast browning beautifully in the oven. On the rack below it she had sweet potatoes baking. Once the turkey was cooked and resting, she'd bake the stuffing and roast the balsamic and olive oil–coated brussels sprouts she'd combined with onions and chestnuts. Already on the table, whole-berry cranberry sauce flavored with orange zest and potato rolls she'd mixed the day before and baked that morning.

Funny thing about life-changing events. Some of them were huge baseball-bat blows to the head, like her parents' deaths. Some of them were little tickles or itches that you didn't notice changing your life until you gained perspective later on. Then there were those in between, like when you went jogging on the beach with your best friend and she made some astute and challenging observations you didn't want to hear, and you realized the new direction was up to you to put into place.

Kendra was making some of those changes now, preparing for others later. She couldn't go on in this limbo— well, she could, but she no longer chose to—of half her old life and half a new one. She could sell the car and buy one that fit her better. She could get a dog and incorporate him or her into her counseling practice, though she'd feel horribly guilty abandoning Byron to days alone in the house at Lena's. She could talk to Matty about putting the house on the market within the next year or two, maybe find out what she'd need to do to fix it up and start working on that now, then eventually look for a new place for herself.

And she could have a lovely Thanksgiving, a day early, with Jameson, without having to intrude on another family's traditions. Tomorrow Kendra planned to spend the morning on the beach and drive up the Pacific Coast Highway in the afternoon. She could choose how she grieved, what she could let go, what she wanted to keep—all the advice she'd been giving other people and not living herself.

As to what she and Jameson would do in the relationship going forward…she'd take Lena's advice and tell him how she felt, even though she hadn't gotten much further than "play it by ear." Breaking off their relationship when he left would be agonizing, but she didn't feel right committing herself to a long-distance romance when she was only just emerging from the worst of her grief and starting to redefine herself.

For all she knew, Jameson wasn't ready to commit either, which would be fine.

Her instinct rolled its eyes. *No, it wouldn't.*

Yes, actually, it would be.

Liar.

Freedom would make it easier to continue rebuilding the life she wanted.

No, it would totally suck.

Stop.

No matter what happened, she and her instinct were going to enjoy the hell out of tonight and however many other times she saw him before he left on Sunday.

The doorbell rang. Kendra broke into a smile, quickly rinsed and dried her hands, then ran to let him in, her heart lifting into its usual joy at the sight of his unbearably handsome face, faltering only slightly when she noticed he'd gotten a haircut—another reminder that he was leaving.

In the next second she noticed his hands behind his back, which he brought forward to offer a bouquet of red roses and a bottle of champagne. "Hello."

"Oh, Jameson, how beautiful. You are spoiling me with flowers. *And* champagne. You are a sweetheart, thank you."

"You're welcome." He walked in, strong and virile, without any limp, and gave her a sweet, lingering kiss. "Mmm. You smell incredible. Is that...turkey?"

"My newest scent." She took the flowers and wine and led the way to the kitchen. "Eau de Thanksgiving."

"Kendra, wow." He took in the food waiting to go into the oven, the table set with her family's china and silver. "This looks amazing."

She found a vase for the roses and took them to the sink, feeling suddenly shy and awkward. "I thought we could have our own Thanksgiving."

"That is a really nice idea. And a lot of work, Kendra. You should have told me, I could have brought something. We could have cooked together."

"You did bring something. Look how beautiful." She put the flowers on the table, which was transformed by their color and elegance. The perfect touch. "I didn't want us to wear ourselves out in the kitchen."

"No?" He came up behind her, drew her back against him. Kendra closed her eyes. His hard body and masculine scent turned her into a giant lust hormone. "Is there another room you'd rather we wear ourselves out in?"

"Hmm." She moved seductively against him, keeping the mood light, not letting the word *leaving* enter her head for more than a second before it was firmly squashed. "I'll give that some thought."

"I think that's a good idea." His lips found the side of her neck; his hands roamed her waist, eventually finding the hem of her shirt and traveling slyly underneath. "Anything in the oven that would spoil in the next half hour?"

Somehow she kept her breathing under control. "Yup."

"Fifteen minutes?"

"Timer's going off in five."

"I'll take that as a challenge."

"Five minutes?" She started to turn but he held her still.

"Shh." His hand was delicious torture on her breasts. The other started a slow journey down her belly. Kendra let her head loll back on his shoulder, prepared to enjoy his touch, then finding herself enjoying more than just his touch. She enjoyed his solid warmth at her back, the strength of the arms around her, the way his breathing changed, betraying his arousal as he concentrated on hers.

The fingers of his right hand inched lower, under the waistband of her shorts—she'd worn a stretch waistband for exactly this reason—then eased under the elastic of her panties. Her own breathing changed, came out in a small burst as he cupped her sex with his warm palm and held her like something precious he wasn't going to let escape.

"Five minutes, Kendra." His voice against her hair was low and full of promise. His fingers began undulating, as if he were playing a scale on a piano, one finger, then the next, playing her so sweetly.

"Mmm, that is nice," she whispered.

"Yeah?" His fingers rose, fell, playing her again, A, B, then C—his middle finger dipped, parting her labia, stroking back and forth before he moved on—D and E, then did the whole thing in reverse. "Four minutes."

"Keep going," she whispered.

His fingers moved again. This time middle C lingered on her clitoris with gentle pulsing presses that made her inhale sharply and hold still, pushing out her hips, wanting him to touch her there again and again.

"Three minutes," he whispered. His hand moved side

to side, fingers trailing in interrupted sequence across her clit, making her work against the need to move as well so at least one finger stayed where she wanted it to.

"Jameson, stay there. *There.* Keep your finger—"

"Two minutes." His knees bent slightly, throwing her off balance. She sagged against him. He supported her easily, now making lazy circles everywhere but where she *wanted* him.

Her breathing grew frantic. She was desperate with desire, feeling half-foolish to be falling apart like this. "Do you realize what you do to me?"

"It goes both ways, sweetheart. One minute."

"I'm not going to make it unless you—"

"You're going to make it." He bent his knees farther; instinctively she stepped one foot out to stay stable, opening herself to him. "Now."

He pushed a finger up inside her, then two, a rhythm that made her cry out until those same fingers returned to her clitoris, slippery with her moisture, and rubbed in earnest, stopping just as her orgasm gathered to slide up inside her again.

She tightened her buttocks, pushed against his fingers.

"Thirty seconds." His arm released her; he supported her with his strong legs like a human chair. His fingers continued making love to her while his other hand reached around to stroke her.

The orgasm gathered again, faster this time, inevitable. She moaned, straining for it, head pushed back against his strong shoulder, fingers clutching his hard biceps.

Ecstasy burned through her in a blissful, powerful wave, blinding her for a few seconds, then crashing over.

Ding ding ding. The timer went off as if she'd triggered it.

Kendra's giggle mixed with her panting, muscles still contracting deliciously around Jameson's fingers. "Made it."

"I knew you would." He helped her stand, get her legs and hips working again. "Is that the turkey?"

"Yes, it needs to come out." She wobbled toward the range, feeling as if her legs were being tried out for the first time. "Because, you know, if meat stays in my hot oven too long, the juices pour out and then it shrinks."

Jameson cracked up. "Wait, that's a *bad* thing? It sounds pretty great to me."

"Bad for turkeys." She sent a lascivious glance at his distorted jeans and took the half breast out of the oven, burnished beautifully brown and smelling like heaven.

"That is a thing of beauty." He cleared his throat pointedly. "So, um, now that the turkey's out, how long until the next thing?"

"The turkey should rest." She threw him a smile, turned up the temperature, slid in the pans of stuffing and brussels sprouts and tossed her oven mitts across the room, where they landed neatly on the counter. "Half an hour."

"I'm thinking a glass of champagne." He crossed to where she'd stood the bottle on the counter.

"I'm thinking the same." She took down flutes from the cabinet near the door to the deck. She'd miss this house. But a new one would be fun to make her own, to fill with her own memories.

A place to share with Jameson when he was in town?

Yeah, sharing tidbits of vacation for the next twenty years. She might as well face it, there was no way they could continue this with anything but frustration and pain.

Stop.

She handed him the flutes with a determined smile. Fun now, serious conversation later.

"I wonder, Ms. Kendra." He twisted off the cork with a loud pop, tipping the bottle to keep the champagne from rushing out. "If you have any objections to drinking this champagne in bed."

"How could *anyone* have objections to drinking champagne in bed?" She picked up the glasses, gave him a come-hither look over her shoulder and headed for her bedroom, hearing him follow, at first at a distance, then closer and closer until she broke, giggling, into a run. "In a hurry?"

He set the bottle on her nightstand, grabbed the glasses from her hand, then tumbled her down on the bed. "Yes."

"What about my champagne?" Her protest was lame; she welcomed him on top of her, closed her eyes, her mind and her heart to how much she would miss him, how deeply she felt about him, and kissed him, wrapping her legs around his thighs, pulling his erection close, feeling it warm and insistent between her legs. She wanted to please him. She wanted him inside her, going crazy from how much he wanted her, how desperately he wanted to come.

And she wanted him to love her, just a little, as she loved him, just a little, even knowing it would make Sunday that much more painful when it came.

No matter what they decided, she'd make sure their parting was beautiful and dignified and something he'd always remember fondly. A tear, a smile, a heartfelt wish for his future happiness, and then she'd hold herself straight, waving until he was out of sight.

After that, she could break down for a while, wallow in her brokenheartedness and then get over it. One thing about surviving tragedy—after the first time it happened to you, and after seeing it happen to so many others, you knew it was not only possible but inevitable to move on and thrive and find happiness again in new and sometimes unexpected places. Spirit the hawk, reborn.

Jameson undressed her slowly, reverently, kissing every inch he uncovered, lingering in places they both liked best. Naked, she pushed him onto his back and did the same to him, dragging her breasts over the firm planes of his chest, her hair over the long hardness of his thighs and her hands and lips over the jutting pride of his erection.

He lay back as she expanded the range of her kisses, across that chest, down his belly, let her mouth hover tantalizingly over his penis before she drew it into her mouth, fisting the base, swirling her tongue around its tip. Jameson's breathing became harsh, labored; his head rolled to one side, eyes closed, brows down, full, sexy lips parted ecstatically. She wanted a picture of him like that to keep by her bed.

Except whomever she made love to next might not appreciate it.

She didn't want to make love to anyone else.

Stop.

She took him all the way in, sucking hard, up and down, a furious denial of her feelings, even knowing there was little point denying them except to make their separation easier.

Jameson clamped a hand on her shoulder, holding her still, then pulled away from her mouth and hauled her up next to him, breathing deeply. "That was close."

"I wouldn't have minded."

"*I* would have minded. We have half an hour. That would have been about three minutes."

"Mmm, good point." She nuzzled his neck, trailing her fingers gently down the soft skin of his penis, loving that contradiction, the erection so hard and masculine and the skin velvety soft and so very sweet.

He lay back again while she idly stroked him, his eyes closed, lips curved in bliss. She studied his face, the high slope of his forehead under the short spikes of his hair. The straight Cartwright nose and high cheekbones, the strong Cartwright jaw. And that soft full mouth, so finely shaped, that called him out of the mold, gave him the look of sensuality his brothers and father lacked.

She'd miss him.

Stop.

She drew her hand up his chest, over to his shoulder, then pushed herself up to straddle him, sliding her sex up and back, pressing his penis flat against his abdomen.

His breath came out in a soft groan. Impressively muscled arms came around her and pulled her down against him; he kissed her hair, her mouth, a long, sweet kiss that made Kendra wrap her arms around his neck and give herself over to it, kiss after kiss, lips clinging, exploring, slow and lovely, involving way too much of her heart.

She loved him.

Oh, hell.

In self-defense she unlocked her arms from around him, rose onto her hands. "Condom?"

He opened his eyes slowly, their clear blue a sudden contrast with his golden skin and the white bed linens around him. "We could go without, Kendra. You're on the pill."

"Pills don't protect against—"

"I tested clean after my last lover."

"I did, too, but there are viruses you can't test for that—"

"Kendra."

Something about the way he said her name stopped her midsentence, made her climb off and sit facing him. "What is it?"

"I want to make love to you. Not just today but for a long time into the future. I'd like us to stay together. I'd like to give this a real shot."

Me, too.

No, it was crazy. But there was no more calling *stop*. They were going to talk about this now, with her Thanksgiving dinner nearly ready and the champagne still untasted.

As if he'd heard her thoughts, Jameson got up, poured them two glasses and handed her one. "Here. Either way you answer, having met you again calls for celebration."

Answer? He hadn't asked her anything. He must mean her reaction to his announcement that they should stay together.

It was impossible.

It was so tempting.

She sipped her bubbly, vaguely noticing the wine was delicious, not able to concentrate fully on enjoying it.

"My future plans have changed."

Kendra was so startled she aborted her next sip. "What do you mean?"

"I'm not extending my commitment to the Air Force."

She stared at him. "What does that mean?"

"It means I'm out after four years. I can come back here to live."

Kendra's heart started beating faster. Four years. That was a lot shorter than twenty. But *four years.* Anything could happen in that time. "You're coming home."

"And I'll be back as often as I can be in the meantime. Depending on your answer."

Answer again. To which question? Would she like that? Would she still be here for him when he visited? Was she happy he was shortening his commitment?

She didn't know. "Jameson, this is a huge change. What does your family think?"

His jaw set. "They'll get over it."

She had to smile. Good for him. Good for Jam-Jam, telling his family what *he* wanted instead of just doing what they did. "I'm proud of you."

"Thanks." He grinned that irresistible grin, sitting naked in her bed, holding a bubbling champagne flute, behind him through huge windows the vista of L.A. and the ocean.

She could keep seeing him. They could turn this relationship into something serious.

No. She didn't want to be serious.

Why not?

She wasn't sure anymore.

"I will never regret the years serving my country or forget what the Air Force has done for me. It's my family I've served for much too long in too many ways." He posed ridiculously, an overbright smile on his face. "This is the start of *me* time!"

Kendra cracked up, nearly spraying champagne over her sheets. "Don't ever say that again."

"Sorry." Jameson gazed at her, his smile gradually fading into something darker and warmer that began a serious spring thaw in her chest. He toasted her with his glass, drained it, then took hers over her protests and put them both on the bedside table. He grabbed his pants and began rummaging in the pocket.

Good boy. Condom. They could put this confusing and uncomfortable conversation on ice while they—

It wasn't a condom he'd pulled out.

Unless they put condoms in jewelry boxes now and she hadn't gotten the memo.

"Kendra."

She sat there, blinking, unable to comprehend what was happening. Maybe it was a necklace? A bracelet? Earrings? A friendship ring?

Depending on her answer. To what question?

"We met under strange circumstances. Twice. The first time was in elementary school when a serious, chubby girl sat next to me and said hello and I threw a spitball at her. The second was in Mike's apartment, when I opened the door to this incredibly funny and beautiful woman and nearly drove her off with my bad mood.

"Matty was right. I've been telling you I love you my

whole life. But I'd like to tell you again, in two different ways. The first is to say it. I love you, Kendra. And the second way is to show you that I always will." He opened the box.

Not earrings.

A ring. A stunning ring of diamond and sapphire chips set in a delicate curve. It was the most beautiful thing she'd ever seen. Her breath came shallow; spots flew in front of her vision. She forced herself to relax, forced her breathing low. The spots cleared.

"This ring symbolizes my promise to you, Kendra. I promise I will always come back to you. I promise that I will work hard to make you proud and I promise that someday I will ask you to be my wife." His mouth curved in a devilish smile. "If you've stopped freaking out by then."

"What?" She jerked her head up from staring at the ring. And freaking out. "I'm not out. Freaking. No."

"You had hard work to do getting me out of my bad mood when we met this second time. I promise also to be that understanding and that determined with you." He touched her cheek, his eyes filled with so much love she could barely look at him.

"Which means, Kendra, when I ask if you'll wear this, I won't let you get away with saying anything but yes."

16

MATTY DROVE EAST on I-10 toward Claremont, having just finished the Wednesday night performance of *Backspace*. She had the next day off for Thanksgiving, which, if tonight went as she hoped, she'd be tempted to skip at Mom and Dad's. Her brothers were bringing girlfriends. This batch of females could surprise her, but so far Mark's and Hayden's judgment of a woman's worth had been based on breasts over brains.

So be it. She'd go of course, if only because she couldn't leave Air Force–ditching Jameson to the wolves by himself.

If tonight went as she hoped.

Part of her was not happy with the chain of events that had led to her change of heart. Part of her felt she should have been able to trust Chris implicitly, and that when he'd insisted nothing had happened with Clarisse six years ago, she should have been able to believe him. But she had been a college kid, on pins and needles from the illicit circumstances of their affair, underexperienced and overwrought. Now, too much pain and time had passed for her to throw it all behind her.

Her relief at finally hearing from Clarisse's mouth the same truth she'd heard from Chris's was so great that she couldn't call it a mistake. Finding out she'd had been in the wrong all these years was remarkably freeing. Going forward, which she desperately hoped they would, she would do whatever she could to prove she trusted Chris now.

A glance at the speedometer made her push her Kia a little faster. She couldn't wait to get to Chris's house and issue a heartfelt apology. And give him the present she'd decided on for both of them. And drag him into bed. And…mmm.

Half an hour later, nearly trembling with excitement, she pulled up opposite his house and switched off the engine, took a little time to sit and think about this moment, six long years after their initial relationship, and how wonderful it was to finally cast off doubt, to stop fighting her feelings for this man, to realize he'd loved her all this time and that it had nearly cost him his sanity to let her go, thinking that doing so would be the best thing for her.

Which, actually, given the possibility of such a happy ending now, it might well have been.

Heart brimming, she patted her jacket pocket to make sure the paper was still there, even though she'd put it in herself an hour earlier and hadn't touched it since. Out of the car, she gazed around her, then up at the stars, inhaling deeply, trying to take everything in, impress each detail onto her memory bank so she could return whenever she wanted.

Heels tapping on the front walk, the sound echoing in the silent neighborhood, she hurried to his front door and rang the bell, unable to keep the smile off her face.

Chris opened, scowling, did a double take, froze in what looked like horror, then swore viciously.

Matty's eyes shot wide. Whatever she'd expected, that wasn't it. "Um. Nice to see you, too."

"I'm sorry, Matty. But my God. Fate is seriously effed up sometimes."

"Chris." She stared at him, taking in his features, his

pallor, the beginnings of fear waking in her system. Was
he ill? "What do you mean?"

He looked at her a moment with pain in his eyes she
didn't understand. Then he stepped back and gestured her
inside.

A woman. A girl. Beautiful. Brunette. Not naked, but
sitting on the couch wearing a low-cut clinging dress short
enough to get her arrested.

"Jenny. This is Matty, who I was just telling you about.
Matty, this is Jenny, who decided to stop by tonight because Satan must have told her you were coming to surprise me, so he could try to ruin my life for the second
time in a decade." He gestured in frustration, hair a rumpled mess, as if he'd been trying to tear it out all night.
In a weird déjà vu moment, she remembered his reaction the first time around, with Clarisse. He'd sounded
the same. Not guilty, not anxious, just pissed off. How
had she missed it?

The problem wasn't with Chris. The problem was with
circumstances and with her.

"Hi, Jenny." Matty kept her voice gentle. Her lips curved
into a smile meant to terrify. Judging by Jenny's deer-in-
the-headlights reaction, it was working. "It's awfully late
to be visiting your professor on a school night, isn't it?"

"I needed to talk to him. He didn't answer his phone."

"Because you never called me." Chris's voice had
calmed some. She glanced at him and saw in his eyes
what she might have been able to see if she'd spared him a
glance six years earlier, if she'd done anything but pour all
her fear and frustration and insecurity over their affair into
anger and blame. Excusable? Yes, actually. Naked women
in your boyfriend's room didn't make cheating an unlikely
conclusion. But she could have taken a second look.

In an ironic flash of insight she recognized now that the

trip to see Clarisse had been a waste of time. Matty would have come to this same place on her own.

She turned back to Jenny. "What did you need him for? Can I help?"

Jenny shook her head, scowl almost as black as Chris's.

"Is there someone else who could help you?"

"I guess."

"Maybe you could go find that person." She smiled even more sweetly. "Right now."

Jenny stood and flounced past them, giving Chris a pleading look on the way out that six years ago would have reduced Matty to furious ash in three seconds. Now she just wanted to roll her eyes.

The door slammed behind her.

"Seems like a lovely girl." Matty turned and gave Chris a thumbs-up, nodding as if they'd just decided to purchase a new car. "Nice legs."

"Mattingly." He closed his eyes and gave a bitter laugh, shaking his head. "I can't tell you what went through my mind when you came to the door."

"Let me guess. 'Uh-oh'?"

"A little stronger."

"I heard some of that."

"Right." He stood straight, hands on his hips, looking so hot in jeans and a blue shirt that she wanted to pounce on him. "She's a nice kid. Bad family situation. I was kind to her. She thought there was more to it than that, apparently."

"Plus you are *so* irresistible."

"Ha." He blew out a shaky breath, looking at her, head tipped to one side. "What's going through your mind, Matty?"

"I wish last time I'd taken a moment to calm down and pay attention. I wish I'd trusted my instinct that what we had was strong instead of wondering how you could ruin it."

"You were young. Too young. I was old enough to take responsibility for how stupid we were being. I should never have let it go so far."

She shrugged. There was no point in blaming anymore. "We were both in it. But yeah, I wouldn't have wanted to keep having to sneak around."

"That was awful."

She nodded, gazing at him, thinking that in a strange sense tonight's timing couldn't have been better. She'd been able to show Chris her trust in a way that would mean a lot more than just telling him.

"So with that hell out of the way, hello, Matty." He dropped a kiss on her mouth, then another, then took her into his arms and kissed her soundly.

"Hi." She sounded like a breathless, ridiculously in love person. Which she was.

"I wasn't expecting you tonight." He kept her close, kissed her temple. "This was a nice surprise."

"I went to see Clarisse."

"Huh." His body stiffened. He took a step back. "Would you like a drink? Because I could use a double."

Matty giggled. "A drink would be really nice."

"Cognac?"

"Perfect."

He strode over to his liquor cabinet in the dining room, poured two healthy shots into balloon glasses and offered her one, gesturing to the couch where Jenny had arranged herself so seductively. "Cheers."

"Cheers." She sipped the fiery sweet liquid. Not yet her favorite, but a lovely indulgence to be drinking with Chris.

"So." He cleared his throat, put his arm along the back of the couch behind her. "What did Clarisse have to say?"

"What I should have known all along. What you kept telling me. That you loved me. That you were never a cheater. That it cost you to let me go, but that you did it for me."

"Thank God." His face relaxed; he closed his eyes briefly. "I was afraid she'd still be lying."

"I shouldn't have had to talk to her." Matty swirled her Cognac, then resolutely met his eyes. "Tonight I would have reacted the same way whether I'd gone to see her or not. It's not nearly enough, but Chris, I am truly sorry I didn't trust you."

"It wasn't our time, Matty." His voice was low, controlled, but the hope in his eyes nearly tore her in half.

She put her glass down and took out the folded paper in her pocket, was about to hand it to him when he took hold of her shoulders.

"I want this to be our time."

She met his kiss, melting into his arms when he wrapped them around her and pulled her into his lap. His mouth was hungry, demanding. Matty answered that hunger and made it clear her body was making demands of its own.

In five minutes their clothes were off and they were straining frantically to join their bodies, giggling when the angles weren't quite on target, when she wasn't quite ready at first, then sighing blissfully when they got it right, when he found her and sank slowly inside. Their eyes met and held, communicating everything they felt for each other.

He moved inside her slowly, holding back, letting their arousal build gradually until they were once again frantic for each other. Matty met and absorbed his thrusts until her own need to come was so strong she couldn't delay anymore, even to keep this beautiful lovemaking going longer.

They'd have time. Years and years…

"Chris," she gasped. "I'm going to come."

He moaned and ground himself into her, pushing her over the edge, then gave the hiss of breath that let her know he'd gone over with her.

Yes. This was their time.

They came down together, releasing the tension, laughing from the sheer physical and emotional joy of what they'd shared. Matty gazed up at him and the words she'd been holding on to for so many years came out as naturally as if she'd been saying them all along. "I love you."

"Aw, Matty." He rolled to one side and pulled her to him tightly. "I've thought about saying that to you again every day for the past six years."

"Say it now."

"I love you." He said it twice more, kissing her, then said it again, "I love you."

"Hmm." Matty grinned at him. "I think this is what happiness feels like."

"I think you're right about that." He pushed back her hair, eyes warm and loving. "And I think you were trying to give me something when I jumped you."

"Oh! Yes!" She struggled up to look around them. "I took it out of my jacket. Where is it? A piece of paper."

"I don't know. Is that…no."

"Did you take it from me?"

"I don't think so." He sat up next to her, scanning the room and their clothes strewn around it. "Maybe it's… No, not here either."

"We'll find it."

"Tell me what it is." He stroked up and down her back.

"A coupon I designed. For a trip for two to Paris." She was brimming with triumph and the pleasure of surprising him. "I sold two houses last week. And we've always wanted to go."

"Matty." He looked stunned, exactly as she'd hoped he would. "That's too much."

"What, you don't want to go to Paris with me?" She shrugged, *oh, well.* "Okay. I can ask someone else."

"Wait, wait, I'll go, I'll go." He shook his head, grinning at her. "If you let me help."

"I want to do this for us."

"But Matty, that's a huge amount of—"

"I know how much it is and I know how much I can afford. Take it or leave it."

He stared at her for a moment, clearly exasperated, then his face cleared. "I'll take it. On one condition."

Matty narrowed her eyes suspiciously. "What's that?"

"That the trip is our honeymoon."

"Our…" She blinked, barely able to take in that he'd just given her all the reassurance she'd ever need, all the love she'd ever want with the only man she'd ever wanted it from. "You…"

"Matty Cartwright." He slid off the couch, got down on his knees and clasped her hands in his, stunningly naked, her man from now until forever. "I have never loved anyone the way I love you. Will you marry me?"

"Yes. Yes. Oh, my gosh, yes." She wrapped her arms around him, pulled his forehead up to hers. "I've always wanted a Paris honeymoon. And I've always and only wanted you."

17

KENDRA STARED GLUMLY at the ceiling, splayed out on her couch with the TV still on. Happy Thanksgiving to her. Nearly noon. She'd been awake from her last fitful doze since six. Hadn't been to the beach. Hadn't organized for a drive up the Pacific Highway. During the past six hours, she had accomplished a couple of trips to the bathroom, one tooth-brushing session, quantity ingestion of junk food and a whole lot of quality angsting.

Jameson had left the beautiful—so, so beautiful!—promise ring in its box by her bed, saying he wanted it staying there to tempt her. Yes, it had tempted her, jumping out of its box and onto her finger about once every ten minutes, until she'd gotten out of bed, driven to the 7-Eleven and bought every type of disgusting, unhealthy food she could find, then returned home and stalked into the living room, determined to escape the diamonds and sapphires taking over her brain.

She wanted to accept the ring. Of course she did. But committing to eventual marriage was a huge step, and she didn't feel she'd known Jameson long enough.

They had fun together, they had similar taste, humor, outlooks, incredible sex. Jameson made her feel beautiful and smart and cherished and sexy as hell. They handled disagreements with care, respect and humor. He made it safe for her to take risks, if that made any sense. In the brief time since she'd known him again she'd realized how much of herself she'd held back, how much she'd been looking to the past instead of the future. Now she was ready to sell her car, get a dog and think about moving out of this house that she loved, but that had never and would never feel as though it belonged to her. Wasn't that enough for commitment?

Yes? No?

Jameson seemed completely sure of her answer, which irritated her. How the hell did he know so much about her and what she wanted and what she was feeling? *She* didn't even know.

Mom and Dad would know. They'd have sensible, practical advice that would make her worries and uncertainty seem silly. They'd say she was overcomplicating a simple yes-no situation. They'd tell her to follow her instinct. And when she told them her instinct was voting both pro and con, they'd insist one side was instinct and one was fear, and help her find out which was which. But Mom and Dad weren't here. Which was probably just as well right now, because they'd have a fit at what she'd been eating.

Not to mention she wanted to be left the hell alone.

The doorbell rang.

Oh, the irony.

She shoved a handful of barbecue-flavor potato chips into her mouth and scowled at the front door.

The doorbell rang again.

"Go away."

Who the hell would show up at her house on Thanksgiving? Lena was with her own family at her sister's house in Santa Monica this year—she was the only friend who'd feel she had the right to show up unannounced on a major holiday. Kendra's clients didn't know her home address.

Jameson was...

Oh, no. Not with her looking like the walking dead. And smelling worse.

She got up and tiptoed to the door just as he started pounding.

"Kendra. It's me, open up."

Kendra groaned. Mr. Macho Military would probably break down the door if she didn't answer. Her car was in the driveway; it didn't take much to figure out she was home.

Wait, she could be on a long walk…

"Kendra." He pounded again. She heard him muttering about going around to look for her in back.

Fine. She opened the door. "Hi."

Jameson turned abruptly and ran back up the steps, his grin widening. He was carrying another beautiful bouquet for her: mixed flowers today, in autumn colors, burgundy, rust and gold. "Happy Thanksgiving, Kendra. You are beyond gorgeous this morning."

She grunted, absurdly glad to see him, but cranky and embarrassed to be caught looking like hell. "What are you doing here?"

"Visiting my true love." He was entirely too cheerful. She might have to slug him. "What are you doing here?"

"Nothing." She took the flowers, stepped back and gestured him in, resigned to him seeing her pigsty.

Oink.

Jameson strode in, then stopped, hands on his hips, and surveyed the living room. Several crushed soda cans littered the coffee table along with the barbecue chips, a Pop-Tarts box, a half-eaten package of Oreos and an empty bag of peanut M&Ms.

As he stared, a throw pillow tumbled off the couch, as if it couldn't bear being seen in such humiliating circumstances.

Kendra knew how it felt.

Jameson turned to her, chuckling. She really would have to slug him. "Have a good night?"

"Best I've had in a while."

"I can see that."

She glared at him. "What are you so happy about?"

"It's Thanksgiving. I'm grateful for many things. My knee recovering, choosing what to do with my life and having the most wonderful woman in the world dying to marry me."

Her hands plonked on her hips. "I am not dying to marry you."

"No?" He drew his brows down. "Well, hey, I know! Let's *talk* about it!"

"I don't *want* to talk. I want you to leave me to my stench."

"Is the living room a good place, do you think? Or the kitchen?"

"Jameson, I think you should—"

"Yeah, I like the kitchen, too, it's brighter." He strode toward it without looking back.

Kendra shuffled behind him, rolling her eyes. He was the most wonderful and annoying person on the planet, and how was she supposed to be dying to marry him when technically he hadn't even *asked* her? He was breaking all rules of politeness and consideration, shoving his way in, talking over her, not listening to what she was saying.

But he looked damn hot. Eyes bright, body filling out neat black pants the way pants should be filled out. His shirt was a rich dark green with a subtle black stripe, his shoulders broad, movements confident and graceful.

Yum.

She laid the flowers on the table, grabbed a vase from the cabinet and arranged them in fresh water. They were gorgeous. And he was sweet to have brought them, especially since he'd only just brought her roses. And she'd been very ungracious to him about it.

"Jameson, I'm—" She broke off at the sight of him sitting calmly at her kitchen table with two stacked pads of paper and a pen in front of him. "What are you doing?"

"Sit." He gestured to the chair opposite. "I have a few questions. I can't stay long, about five more minutes. I promised to help Mom in the kitchen."

"What questions? What is this?" She scowled her way to the chair he'd indicated and slouched into it, scratchy and hot.

"Tell me what you're feeling." He looked up, all impish seriousness, pen poised to record her answer.

Kendra narrowed her eyes. "Are you making fun of me?"

"Yup."

"You have no clipboard."

"I know." He shook his head in disgust. "I'm an amateur. But a serious amateur. Feelings?"

"Okay." She thunked her elbows on the table, chin flanked by her fists. "Troubled. Confused. Lethargic."

"Appetite okay?"

"As long as the food isn't healthy."

"Sleeping well?"

"No."

"Sexual appetite?"

"Um. That seems to have perked up lately."

"How lately?"

"Like…in the last five minutes."

A brief smile sneaked onto his face. "Hmm. We'll take that into consideration."

"We?"

"Me and my questions. Let's see…any major gifts of jewelry recently?"

She snorted. "Yes."

"Any urges to buy a pet?"

"Yes."

"Desire to trade in your current vehicle?"

"Yes again."

"Uh-huh. Uh-huh." He tapped the pencil against the

pad. "I think I'm getting the picture. Oh, and speaking of pictures, I brought the ones I drew on Rat Beach."

"Jameson, thank you." Pleasure jolted her out of her bad mood, at least temporarily. She was curious to see what he'd done.

"I'll leave them with you since I need to go. But before I do, I have one more question. Very important."

"Uh-oh." She narrowed her eyes. "What's that?"

"Kendra Lonergan." He leaned forward, touched her cheek gently. "What are you most afraid of?"

JAMESON PUSHED BACK his plate, leaving his last few bites of pecan pie untouched. He'd had enough—of food and family. As usual his father and brothers had dominated the meal, while Matty and Mom had listened in annoyance, amusement or some combination. His brothers had hooked up with a new crop of women beautiful to look at and tedious to listen to. Every now and then one of the men would get in some "funny" dig about Jameson not making a career of the Air Force. Matty and Mom would look uncomfortable. The boobsy twins would laugh. The topic would change, then return.

A few weeks ago the teasing would have made him miserable. Now? He just nodded, smiled, acknowledging the jokes but not commenting or defending himself. He didn't have to. He no longer cared what they thought of his life decisions. He could love his family without being victim to their…Cartwrightness.

And he had somewhere else to feel accepted as he was.

The burn in his chest that had become his constant companion became stronger. Thrill and fear. For all his supposed confidence that Kendra would stay with him, for all his belief that their love was the real thing and would survive the next four years and on until death, he could answer that favorite last question of Kendra's easily now, the one he'd turned on her.

His biggest fear? That she wouldn't give them a chance. That she'd need someone right here, who could reassure her every day in his arms, in his bed that he was not going to leave her, not going to disappear.

Jameson couldn't offer her that now. And he couldn't ask her to pick up her life and hard-won practice and start over now and every other time the Air Force moved him.

The doorbell rang, stopping Mark from recounting every detail of some reality show he'd been watching the night before.

"Who could that be?" Katherine rose from the table.

"Aunt Bea?" Hayden suggested.

Jameson groaned silently. God, no.

"She's in Missouri with a friend who isn't well," Jeremiah announced.

"Oh, yes, yes, hello, come in. Nice to see you." Katherine's voice grew louder from the foyer. A musical female voice answered her.

Jameson stood, eyes trained on the dining room door, aware that everyone at the table was staring at him.

Kendra. She stepped into the dining room and so far into his heart that he thought it was going to stop beating.

"Hello, everyone." She gave a huge smile, looking cool and beautiful in a room of stuffed, bored and lethargic people. About as far from the way she'd looked at home that morning as she could get. It even seemed she'd brought in fresher air. Her gaze met Jameson's; her smile widened. "Sorry to interrupt your dinner."

He shook his head, trying to communicate his pleasure at seeing her without making his brothers start gagging. "I was just finished."

"Would you like some pie, Kendra?" His mother was already at the china cabinet looking for another plate.

"No, no, I already ate, thank you." She winked at him, knowing he was picturing Pop-Tarts, then went around the room introducing herself, charming each of the men in his family. Hayden cracked up. Mark blushed. His father took her hand and held it longer than was appropriate. Even the girlfriends smiled approvingly. Matty gave her a huge hug, beaming. Jameson was happy for Matty, though he still owed Chris a punch in the face. Maybe at the altar.

"I get it now." Dad brought his hand down on the table. "This beautiful woman is the reason you're quitting the Air Force, Jameson."

"I'm afraid I am." Kendra laughed easily. "In four years we plan to join a commune in North Dakota to raise goats and llamas. I'm already carrying his triplets."

Her smile continued to shine through the atmosphere of sudden horror in the room. Finally Matty couldn't suppress her laughter anymore; eventually, even the boobsy twins got it.

Jameson walked to Kendra and put his arm around her. "We do have news."

He felt her stiffen. "What are you doing?"

Jameson squeezed her shoulder. "About another commitment I've made."

"Jameson." Her furious whisper made him chuckle.

"I promised to spend the afternoon with Kendra at her place." Beside him Kendra went limp with relief.

"You won't stay for pie?" Jameson's mom had finally found a plate.

"No, really, thank you, Mrs. Cartwright." Kendra smiled brilliantly and kicked Jameson in the shins. "I just came to kidnap your son."

"Well, all right." His mom grinned at him, looking much younger than her fifty years, and walked them to the door amid a chorus of goodbyes and wishes of happy

Thanksgiving. Jameson didn't think he'd ever left his family feeling so warm and fuzzy.

Kendra was a miracle.

The door closed behind them. Four steps later, Kendra turned and threw herself at him at the same time he threw himself at her. Their kisses were deep and desperate, arms tight around each other, pelvises pressed close.

One of the windows in the dining room grated open.

"Hey, get a room." Hayden's voice, booming out into the front yard.

Jameson chuckled and gave him a brotherly finger, then pulled Kendra down the front walk toward her car.

"Your brothers are charming as ever," Kendra said dryly.

"Aren't they?" He followed her around to the driver's side and pressed her against the door, kissing her with more appetite than he'd had for his dinner. It had to mean something that she'd shown up today. That she'd introduced herself to his family. That she seemed so cheerful and calm, all while carrying triplets. He wanted to ask what she'd decided—hell, he wanted to demand she marry him right now. But this was her kidnapping, so he'd let her take the lead.

"Where are you taking me to?"

"My house."

"Yeah?" He leaned back slightly to get a better look at her green-eyed, auburn-haired beauty, keeping his hips pressed tightly to hers. He was still half-erect from their passionate kisses. "What are we going to do there?"

"You'll see."

"I think I'm going to like this."

"I think you are, too." She tipped her head back; her eyes went past him. Her breath caught.

"What is it?" Jameson peered into the sky and saw a red hawk swooping over their heads.

"Nothing." She laughed softly. "Reminds me of an old friend."

"You have bird friends?"

"Don't you?" She snapped out of her trance and opened her car door. "Let's go. Silly to drive less than a mile, but I wanted to get you back fast."

"Ah, so this is urgent?" He slid into the passenger side.

She flashed him a sultry-eyed look that made his half erection go for three-quarters. "Very."

"I understand. I'm pretty sure I can help you with whatever you need."

Kendra squeezed his hand, then put the pedal down and drove like a wild woman until they reached her driveway, where she bounced to a stop.

"I'm going car shopping tomorrow. Want to come?" She opened the door and jumped down.

"Absolutely." He was already out, hurrying her to the front door, both of them giggling like idiots.

Inside, their mouths joined; they moved together toward her room, shedding clothes along the way.

Naked, they fell onto the bed, tangling their limbs, touching and writhing to be closer, then closer still.

Crap. He pulled his mouth off hers. Immediately Kendra started in on his neck. "No condom."

She pulled away slightly, started exploring between his legs with her hand, fisting his cock, reaching past it to stroke his balls. "Don't need one."

His brain went blank. No, no, he had to think…

"Why don't we need one?"

"Because I say so."

He rolled his eyes, grabbed her hands, pinned them above her head and lunged over her. "Really? Is that how things will be from now on? How *you* say?"

"Uh-huh." She blinked sweetly at him. God, he loved her. "For instance. You're going to slip inside me right now just the way you are, and feel me around your cock, all naturally hot and wet."

Jameson swallowed. "Ungh."

"Then you'll start moving and be able to feel me gripping you." She lifted her head and dragged the tip of her tongue slowly across his lips. "Really tightly."

He shifted on top of her, breathing hard, the tip of his penis planted at the juncture of her tightly closed thighs.

"Then I'll whisper what I want you to do to me tomorrow, and the next day, until you can't take it anymore and explode inside me."

"Yes." He sounded desperate. Because he was.

She spread her legs slowly. Jameson lifted to look down at her sex, so sweetly formed and so inviting, all reddish-brown curls and lush pink lips. He couldn't get enough— wouldn't get enough for a long time, if ever. Not using a condom must mean she'd decided to accept the ring and all it symbolized. He wanted to hear her say it.

But he'd play this game her way.

Slowly he slid inside her, and without the barrier of the condom her flesh was as slick and warm as she'd promised and embraced him like the world's most sensual glove.

Within three minutes he knew he was not going to be able to last, that he was going to come too soon for her to be ready. He gritted his teeth and held on to her buttocks, forced his body to go still.

"What is it?"

"I'm too close."

"Yeah?" She started pushing up and down, then lifted one leg nearly up to his shoulder, increasing the pressure.

"Kendra." He was practically going blind from lust. "If you do that—"

"Oh, but I *am* doing that, Jameson."

She was. It was too much. He groaned and thrust into her; the orgasm swept him like a hurricane, leaving him flattened and powerless, overwhelmed by the physical and emotional power of what lay between them. She had to know how he felt.

"I love you." He murmured the words into her neck. He didn't care if she didn't answer, he just wanted her to know.

She was doing something. He couldn't tell what. He couldn't lift his head. It was all he could do to keep breathing.

"Jameson," she said softly. "Look."

He dragged himself up to peer at her, blinking stupidly, then followed her gaze.

His ring. She was wearing his ring.

Energy flooded back into his body. He held her hand, gazing at the stones, so perfect on her slender finger. "Kendra."

"I love you too, Jameson." Her eyes were sweet green, shining, melting him. "I'll be proud to wear this."

He kissed her, holding her, tasting every inch of her beautiful lips until finally, remarkably, he wanted to talk to her more than he wanted to kiss her. "What changed your mind?"

"Two things, actually. First, that picture you drew of me in high school." She tipped her head, looking at him with awe. "You really saw me. You remembered me. That was…amazing."

"I've kept you in my head all these years." He traced her beautiful mouth with his finger. "I've loved you all my life."

"I didn't know."

"Worm sandwich, Kendra…" He laughed with her, happier than he could ever remember being. "And reason two?"

"Believe it or not, that question, what did I fear the most. I'd been going back and forth and over and under our situation, making myself crazy. But once I was able to sit alone and really consider my answer—it was so obvious." She touched his face tenderly. "My greatest fear was losing you. I realized that if losing you was my worst fear, then the only thing I should be worried about was keeping you."

He kissed her, kissed her again and again, lowering her back down to the mattress to kiss her better. And then even so soon after his climax, he started adding hot thoughts to the loving ones and moved down to make sure she enjoyed this time in bed as much as he had. This time and every time, stretching ahead for four tough years apart—but then the rest of their lives together.

As his tongue entered her and he felt her shuddering response, he knew she was made for him and he was made for her.

Afterward, they lay in a blissful haze of joy, stroking, touching, planning, daydreaming about their future.

"Will you come with me to the Humane Society in the morning, Jameson? I've decided in order to survive your absence I need company in the house."

"Sure, of course." He'd walk on coals for her—but the Humane Society would be less painful. In fact, he loved the idea of doing a domestic errand with her. "What kind of dog were you thinking about getting?"

"Well…" She stretched luxuriously against him, a mischievous smile growing on her gorgeous face. "I've given it a lot of thought, what kind would work with my lifestyle and how Byron would feel about being replaced. It wasn't until last night when I sorted myself out about you that I realized. This animal would belong to you, too. Then the obvious solution came to me."

"What's that?"

She reached to squeeze his injured knee gently, grinning sweetly. "I'm going to buy us a cat."

* * * * *

REQUEST YOUR FREE BOOKS!
2 FREE NOVELS PLUS 2 FREE GIFTS!

HARLEQUIN
Blaze®
red-hot reads!

YES! Please send me 2 FREE Harlequin® Blaze™ novels and my 2 FREE gifts (gifts are worth about $10). After receiving them, if I don't wish to receive any more books, I can return the shipping statement marked "cancel." If I don't cancel, I will receive 4 brand-new novels every month and be billed just $4.74 per book in the U.S. or $4.96 per book in Canada. That's a savings of at least 14% off the cover price. It's quite a bargain. Shipping and handling is just 50¢ per book in the U.S. and 75¢ per book in Canada.* I understand that accepting the 2 free books and gifts places me under no obligation to buy anything. I can always return a shipment and cancel at any time. Even if I never buy another book, the two free books and gifts are mine to keep forever.

150/350 HDN F4WC

Name _____

(PLEASE PRINT)

Address _____ Apt. # _____

City _____ State/Prov. _____ Zip/Postal Code _____

Signature (if under 18, a parent or guardian must sign)

Mail to the **Harlequin® Reader Service:**
IN U.S.A.: P.O. Box 1867, Buffalo, NY 14240-1867
IN CANADA: P.O. Box 609, Fort Erie, Ontario L2A 5X3

Want to try two free books from another line?
Call 1-800-873-8635 or visit www.ReaderService.com.

* Terms and prices subject to change without notice. Prices do not include applicable taxes. Sales tax applicable in N.Y. Canadian residents will be charged applicable taxes. Offer not valid in Quebec. This offer is limited to one order per household. Not valid for current subscribers to Harlequin Blaze books. All orders subject to credit approval. Credit or debit balances in a customer's account(s) may be offset by any other outstanding balance owed by or to the customer. Please allow 4 to 6 weeks for delivery. Offer available while quantities last.

Your Privacy—The Harlequin® Reader Service is committed to protecting your privacy. Our Privacy Policy is available online at www.ReaderService.com or upon request from the Harlequin Reader Service.

We make a portion of our mailing list available to reputable third parties that offer products we believe may interest you. If you prefer that we not exchange your name with third parties, or if you wish to clarify or modify your communication preferences, please visit us at www.ReaderService.com/consumerchoice or write to us at Harlequin Reader Service Preference Service, P.O. Box 9062, Buffalo, NY 14269. Include your complete name and address.

HB13R2